# CRAWLSPACE

# THE INSECURITY TRIPTYCH
## THREE NOVELLAS. THREE SECURITY GUARDS.
## THREE NIGHTMARES.

### PROVOCATION

Anorexia nervosa survivor Madeleine Kyle embodies twenty-one years of medical intervention; a complex system of internal rules to navigate the dark tides of her fate. When she is stalked by a Library security guard, Madeleine is pushed to the depths of her unique psyche. In a violent endgame, meaning and motive are as murky as the depths of a river in flood.

### THE CENTRE

Zilla Bannich is a dark haired, thick-thighed Polish-Australian misfit on the Gold Coast. As a shopping centre security guard, Zilla is first-on-scene to an incident—a child abandoned, a mother abducted—but falls under suspicion as she clumsily taints the evidence and appears to know the child. *The Centre* explores unspoken truths of girlhood and the erotic passion of belonging, leading us to consider the freedom of love in liminal spaces.

### CRAWLSPACE

In 1987, baby Marlene witnesses her father mutilated in a Port Moresby compound invasion, giving rise to a deep psychological scar and a powerful family secret. Twenty-five years later, Marlene finds her perfect match in depressed outer-suburban Brisbane. Andy is a Visa-dependent teenage American escaping his past, and a cyber-security guard who can lay his hands on your money anytime he chooses. An unplanned pregnancy gives urgency to Marlene and Andy's next scam. But who is it that watches from the crawlspace under their humble house of dreams?

# CRAWLSPACE

## INSECURITY TRIPTYCH #3

MEG VANN

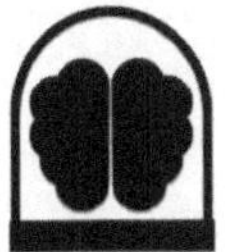

Brain Jar Press
PO Box 6687
Upper Mt Gravatt, QLD, 4122
Australia
www.BrainJarPress.com



Cover design by Peter Ball
Cover Images: *Workman with protective suit crawling under house from crawlspace,* Vineyard Perspective/Shutterstock

ISBN: 978-1-922479-47-1 (Print); 978-1-922479-46-4 (Ebook)

I.

The gunmetal snake rested under a pile of rotting wood. Its slender coils tensed as a larger body slid past, forming wide dirt tracks through the cobwebbed crawlspace.

Two pairs of eyes, shining in the shadows. Watching.



An anonymous white sedan crawled up the deserted street, arcing past the guardhouse to dock in the driveway of a locked carport. The compound at 57 Boroko Place was one of the smaller ones; no dogs, no concrete, no pool. But like all compounds in Port Moresby, it boasted a twenty-four-hour guard and a tall fence topped with razorwire.

Terry felt like a king every time he came home to it, and then, as he locked the garage behind him, he wondered if kings always felt this fucking guilty. It was nearly dark. Dionne would be getting anxious, and he would pay the price for her fears in ear leather. His dirt-encrusted boots crunched across the floodlit dead zone to the front door of number 5, twinned in a double-storey unit at the far end of the block with the recently vacated number 4.

At thirty-five, Terry had finally taken the plunge. Married the pretty lady who regularly kept him company when he was PNG-side. Welcomed a daughter into the world four months later. Set up home in Moresby—the furthest he could convince his new wife to stray from the infinitely extended Kwan family in Lae. A white Australian miner marrying a coffee-baron's knocked-up daughter? They were officially ostracised. But Terry knew that for Dionne and her womenfolk, it was mostly business as usual, in and out of each other's homes as often as time and unreliable transport would allow.

Terry was almost certain the baby girl was his—her grey eyes gazed up at him, serious and curious—and even if she wasn't, he didn't really care. Something about this whole domestic arrangement suited him. The day-to-day rhythms of fatherhood anchored his restless spirit; calmed the pale demon flames of malcontent that had chased him around the rich mines of the South Pacific his whole adult life.

For now, at least.

'Psssh! Baby sleep.' Dionne hissed at Terry to hush, hurrying towards him as he stepped through the door, then closed and locked it behind him. She raised her eyes and lips; a quick kiss and a light slap on his chest. 'You're filthy!'

A laugh rumbled up through Terry's beard. 'Yeah, I am a filthy fellow, my little darlin'. I'm your filthy, filthy husband.' He wrapped himself around her and pressed her tight to his grubby shirt, knowing it would both offend and delight.

She wriggled in Terry's arms. 'No, you'll wake *Baobei*.'

'Is Maria still here? What's for tea?'

'Maria comes nine to two, you know.' Dionne rolled her eyes, extricating herself from his affections. 'I'll make sausage.'

'Chinese or Aussie?'

She flicked her hair and headed off into the kitchen. 'Chinese, of course. Aussie sausage too *small*.'

Terry climbed the stairs and spent a pleasurable half-hour in the shower. Fresh towels, clean clothes, all neatly stacked and folded by old Maria's deft hand. Maria, a loyal and beloved Kwan *haus meri*, came with Dionne: a package deal that suited Terry well.

He ran his rough palms down over his belly, hairy and round

but firm as silverside. He stepped into his favourite pair of faded elastic-waist shorts, looking forward to his night: a feed and a beer, then fire up the amp for a few hours and put that new Fender through its paces. Maybe, if Dionne was up for it, get some head. The baby fairly tore her a new one; he accepted it might be a while before she could offer the full menu.

A dull thud reverberated through the night. Terry felt more than heard it, floorboards shuddering beneath his bare feet. Shorts still half-mast, he jerked forward but overbalanced, crashing into the corner of the wooden bed.

'Argh, fuck!' He lurched upright. Pain tore through his hip. He wrenched up his shorts, his back prickling with adrenalin. He grabbed his farm gun and a few shells from the unlocked toolbox under in their bed.

A rumbling echoed through the night, like tanks on the move. Punctuated by gunshots: one, two, three-four-five. But there were no tanks in Moresby, just angry mobs. Raskols, warring tribes, corrupt cops.

Terry raced to the nursery. Dionne was there already, grabbing the tiny pink bundle from the cot, clutching her tight. She turned to him, eyes sparking panic. 'Out the back. Very close!'

'Grab your bag. Wait by the side door.' He gripped her shoulder, squeezed. 'In the cupboard. And keep Marly quiet.'

Dionne gave a short nod and vanished down the hall. Terry ran down the stairs and out to the back porch, temples pounding with rage. He forced himself to stop at the top of the short flight of steps leading to the backyard. Drew a long, narrow breath into the rigid barrel of his chest, and sent his senses out into the humid night.

Burning rubber stung his eyes, but that was nothing new for payday Friday. Maybe the danger was passing already—no more shots, only breaking glass splintering in the distance. He waited a minute, fingering the ammo in his pocket, constantly surveying the treed skyline for a telltale orange glow.

The grumble of sticks and fists banging on compound fences grew quieter, subsonic. Off to ruin someone else's night. A few minutes later, the sounds faded away completely. The sullen silence draped like jungle vines over his street once more—rows of houses, cleaved by razor wire, conjoined in the defiance of the damned.

Nick, the night guard, strode past. Gun drawn, checking the perimeter. He spied Terry and raised his hand, pushing down on an invisible lever—*go back inside*.

As Terry turned back to his wife and daughter, he made up his mind. Dionne would just have to see sense. This fucking country could blow itself apart for all he cared, but it sure as hell wasn't going to take that little grey-eyed girl with it.

### One year later, Port Moresby, PNG

Terry's eyes flicked open, senses alert. He had heard something. Lava shot through his veins, heart beating so hard his chest jumped. He battled REM-dead muscles, zombie slow as he craned his head around and checked the doorway.

He could make out the familiar shapes of their bedroom, but strange shadows loomed all around. The dead of night pressed on his sockets, pupils straining to let in enough light. Finally, he identified the foreign angles as packing boxes, filled and stacked and ready to go.

Nothing there, just walls and doorways and cartons, shadow on shadow on shadow.

He let out a slow breath, and turned back to check on Dionne. She lay sleeping, a sand-dune silhouette on the other side of the bed. His system powered down a little, enough to realise a nasty hangover was stalking him.

Terry pressed his palms to his tender temples. Water. He needed water. He swung his legs over the side of the bed, repressing a groan for Dionne's sake as gravity squeezed his sorry head. Yeah. It had been a pretty good party: their grand farewell. Dozens of Kwans, from frail old *jo-mo* to a clutch of noisy kids who had to be watched like hawks around little Marly. Another dozen of his workmates and their wives. During their time in Moresby, Dionne had made friends with a couple of them. Sort of. They liked to stick with their own, the ex-pats, and Dionne's reluctance to leave stood her apart from the ladies who were just making the best of a lucrative situation; trading security for luxury, convenience for adventure, and biding their time until they could haul their families safely back home to Oz.

*Good riddance, Pinji.* The soles of Terry's feet were satin dry, slipping on the floorboards, and he put one hand on the wall for balance as he shuffled to the bathroom in the dark.

Then he heard it again. *Thunk.* The sound of a drawer closing? Terry's blood fizzed with fear.

The noise—it came from the nursery.

He took a step backwards, shielding his body behind the frame of the bathroom door, bending forward just enough to peer with one blurry eye down the room opposite.

A minute passed, then two. Outside, areca palms shushed against bar-brindled windows. Time stretched thin and brittle with half-formed terrors.

Silence echoed through the apartment like an empty church. Terry's pulse slowed again. All was still and quiet, but he would take a quick reccy, just to reassure himself. He debated going for his gun, but decided against it. Just a false alarm, and he was probably too shaky to load it anyway. He moved out from behind the bathroom door. First to check the nursery, where the door stood wide open. Then he'd go down to the kitchen, scout around, find some damn codeine, and get back to sleep. The stress of moving, of arguing with Dionne and her family, everything—his nerves were clearly fucked.

He reached the nursery door, warm joy washing over him as he saw the cot undisturbed, the room fairly humming with the blissful peace that surrounds a sleeping baby. Tracing night shadows with his gaze, he noted the change table, crisp and white, the set of drawers so tiny that he couldn't open them without toppling everything off—towers of carefully stacked nappies, tubs of talc and pawpaw ointment and who knows what. Dionne would hiss at him, *leave it,* then pass him the clean sweet bundle when she was all done.

Something snagged his gaze. One of the drawers was askew

on its runners, as if closed in a hurry. He frowned, squinted into the dim recess between the table and the cot. A slipshod bundle of clothes rested on the floor. It wasn't like Maria to leave things untidy—she must have been busy, getting everything ready for the move, and helping out with the party, too. But then, he thought he'd heard the women planning to pack the baby's room tomorrow—today—while he manhandled the boxes into the garage, ready for collection. So what was that mess of cloth on the floor, piled up right next to the wooden slats of Marly's cot? He peered into the washing bundle more closely.

And then, it moved. The crumpled shadow shifted, so slightly that Terry wasn't sure of his own senses, even while his legs twitched with panic. He took a tentative step forward into the room. Compound safety guidelines streamed like wraiths through his mind—never respond to an invasion threat alone— he must leave, call for help, get back-up.

But he was in the nursery, and that bundle may or may not have moved, and his vision was rapidly staining blood-red with protective rage. His fists clenched, his breathing stopped, his bones forged into steel with the might of love. One more step forward.

The pile of clothes exploded into the form of a man, crouching at the end of the cot, thin and gangly as an orb spider. Harsh fumes strafed the room; paint, petrol, glue. The man's eyes were utterly blank.

Terry's mind honed to one sharp, primal instinct. His thick torso jerked forward. His fingers clutched the night air like a weapon.

A tense, high-pitched growl warned him off. The intruder slowly raised his right arm. It telescoped out until it was twice the length of any man's.

Terry's blood froze. The bush knife reached halfway across the room, pointing straight up at his beard. He clamped his teeth on an impulse to bellow. He could not wake the baby. He could not draw his wife into danger. He realised he was blocking the intruder's only means of escape, but he would not back away. He could not leave his daughter.

He could only attack.

Terry charged at the man. He was twice the intruder's size, and monstrous with noiseless rage. He shoved the knife-hand down and away, but it slashed against his thigh. That's when the first lash opened his skin, but it was nothing. Nothing, compared to the life of his daughter. His pulled the intruder up by hic shirt and slammed his fist into the man's face again and again. His bare knuckles split against teeth and bone. The man slumped over the end of the cot.

The blood from his thigh pumping hot and slick, Terry staggered towards his daughter, his fingertips barely making contact with her soft pyjamas before the knife was back, this time at Terry's throat. He blocked it and pulled the intruder in close against his chest, forcing both men away from the cot. The man's eyes were inches away from his face. They flickered with a sudden flare of life. The blade slashed down across Terry's jaw, bouncing off his collarbone before it found purchase. It split his tough hide, sliced through muscle and cartilage, and wedged into his shoulder joint. Blood leaked out. Terry reached up his other hand to pull it free, but the blade stuck fast. The intruder tugged and wrenched at the handle. Terry roared with pain. Both men fought to get the knife under control. Terry lost his grip on the handle and instinctively shoved the intruder away with such force Terry heard his body hit the far wall with a whump.

Terry's shoulder was now pumping out blood. Shadows ate up his vision, strobing in black and white flashes. The last flash he saw burned into his brain: baby Marlene pulling herself upright by the bars of her cot, her bunny pyjamas fingerpaint stained with his blood.

He was blind when he heard the gunfire. Blind when hot liquid iron drenched face and chest. The shot was so close it blew out his hearing. He raked his fingers across his eyes and caught a glimpse of the room.

The gun clattered to the floor as Dionne collapsed behind them, keening in shock. Oil-black pools formed and mingled around the men, entwined, unmoving, on the nursery floor. The night watched in hot, close silence as the blood-spattered baby girl stood up in her cot and screamed, and screamed, and screamed.


Logan hospital, 1992.

With one hand, Dionne slapped through the double doors of the rehab suite at Logan Hospital, her pregnant belly a tight ball of muscle balanced on her slim frame. Her other hand was clasped around the wrist of a nearly four-year-old Marlene in tow.

'Is he finished?' She looked around the room, empty but for the strange heavy shapes and walking aids they made her husband use over and over until tears muddied his beard.

A single nurse approached from the far corner, clipboard in hand. 'Can I help?'

'Where is my husband?' Dionne's heart shrank. She'd been through this before. She knew where he would be, and she didn't want to know.

'Ah, Mrs Hatchier, I'm sorry.' And this one actually sounded sorry, unlike the one last week, last month, last year. 'Mr Hatchier has been taken up for further tests. The—complications—with his medicine are making the rehabilitation regime tricky to get right.'

'He has to get better. Get to work. We cannot live like this, him always at hospital, always sick, more tests.'

'The doctors are doing their best to get the dose right, but so much of it depends on the patient's behaviour at home. Is your husband, ah, taking any additional medication?'

'How do I know what he does? Every morning I measure his pills, I watch him take them, I check his hiding spots. But I'm at work all day. He watches Marly. You want a child to play doctor then? You want to give her your clipboard with all our business in it?'

Marlene, lumpen quiet as ever, pulled on Dionne's arm by sinking her weight towards the ground. This was Marly's main way of communicating—not so much with words as with her body, pushing and pulling against Dionne until she wanted to scream. But Dionne never screamed, never pushed back, only gave her daughter patience, if not understanding. 'Yes, Marlene, what do you want?'

'Why Da sick?'

'Huh?' Surprised, Dionne bent down, bending her knees carefully to balance her changed centre of gravity. The child had shown no sign of noticing her father's ill health until now: as far as Marlene knew, all fathers were like hers. 'What?'

'Why Da sick again?'

'He will get better soon, Marlene.'

'But Da sick again, and—', her face crumpled, voice growing louder, 'just, just… *why?*'

It was time. The moment fell on mother and daughter like a sodden cloak: the moment Dionne had feared as she part-paid bills and hustled cleaning jobs; the moment creating disturbances in her busy periphery as her husband's addictions take shape and charge the child like a wild boar. Through the wakeful nights, her memories of servants and fresh towels twice daily and mealtime menu selections spun like lanterns casting her thoughts into chaos. She would shift her heavy belly from side to side and ruminate on how her fate, seeking a way back to her lost future, desperate for a way to save the family's face and arse at the same time. So, as this moment landed, she reached for a cover story and found it fully formed, utterly convincing, locked and loaded like that old farm gun.

Dionne knelt in front of Marlene, placing a firm hand on her daughter's tensed shoulder, and bestowed this story as if arming her with a shield.

'Da was in an accident. He fell down. He fell down the mine and hurt his shoulder and his leg. That is why your Da needs hospital, medicine. Why he sleeps in the day and calls out at night.' She saw the nurse open her mouth, snapped upright and held up a hand, *stop*. 'But he will get better, Marlene. He will get better and take care of us again.'

The image of blood on her baby's face was only ever an eye blink away: that one gunshot had changed her from a soft, spoilt girl into a hard-shelled woman. How had it affected that baby girl, seeing such things before she could even talk?

Dionne's stomach clenched tight around the *Baobei* on the way. With each new hardship, she toughened, like chicken too long on the grill. She didn't like it, and she couldn't change it. But she could protect her daughter from it.

And so, she stared into Marlene's grey eyes, willing her to forget, to take up this story like a shield against the awful truth of that night. 'Da will get better and take care of us, like he used to. Like he promised.'

Relief dulled the girl's fear-bright eyes. For the first time since Dionne's belly grew big, Marly offered her soft, sqaure paw into her mother's calloused palm. 'Okay, Ma, okay.'


Wonglepong, Queensland, 1995.

Seven years old, Marly kept her precious things in a shoebox under her bottom bunk. The cardboard had a shiny blue coating and a picture of sensible shoes like Ma wore, but Marly had scratched over them with zigzag lines that spelled out secret messages only she could understand. Inside? A prized, heavy porcelain doll with ruined blonde hair and eyes that opened and shut, *nighty-night*, when you tipped her head. Next to her, a rubber ball covered with stubbly spikes that made it so easy to throw and catch. A purple pencil and matching sharpener and a rubber that smelled like grape lollies—all three teasures nicked, one by one over a two-week campaign, from Tess who sat beside her in school. No one was allowed to touch her precious things, especially not her sister, who had just got her very own toy car for her teddy to drive: brand new too, not smudged or with bits missing like Marly's stuff.

But now, the grape-shaped rubber had teeny, tiny bite marks, and a piece missing.

'Juny!' Marly screamed her sister's name. 'Stay out of my things!'

Scramble bump bang, Juny was out the door and down the steps and into the backyard. Marly followed, ready to launch.

But Ma was in the kitchen, in her cleaning uniform and getting ready to leave for work. Da was there too, drinking beer on the back deck. They both turned to her with matching frowns, one hazy, one laser focussed.

And so, she slowed to a stroll and smiled at her sister over the railings. 'Wanna play outside?'

Sitting in the dirt-packed backyard, Marly was quiet a while, watching Juny and rubbing her hands back and forth across the fine grey dust either side of her crossed legs, grit in the folds at her knees, black stripes in the creases around her toes. Her palms tingled, sending a hungry ache up her arms and into her chest and belly and somewhere else; lower, deeper.

She glanced up at the deck again. Da was standing so that his shade fell across Ma, making her disappear. He had that look, like Ma was doing the wrong thing again. She never got his medicine just right—he always had to tell her *more, now* and she would say not yet, and he would blow up like a storm and whip around until he died out on the couch, hogging it, twitching and sweating, so the girls couldn't even watch *My Little Pony* in peace.

Ma was always working; Da was always sleeping.

Juny, only three, practically still a baby, was pulling paspalum blades out from their green tubes. She would tug and tug and break it off, frowning at the short dry stem in her hands.

'Like this, dummy.' Marly gripped a blade of grass, ran her thumb nail down the stem until she felt the rim of outer leaves, then pressed and pulled—firm and gentle. 'Like a Christmas cracker. Pull too soft, you lose. Pull too hard—', she shrugged, '— you lose.' She stuck the resulting straw straight into the gap between her middle teeth, nibbling until sweet sap moistened her tongue.

Juny rolled onto her belly, reaching for the juicier clump of grass near Marly's ankle. She felt for the ridge of leaf that signalled the lighter green stem within, and carefully pulled. 'It a tough one, Marly.'

Marly leaned over and tugged it out easily. She looked down at Juny, always watching her big sister with those trusting brown eyes. Marly lifted the straw of grass slowly to her own mouth, teasing.

'No-no-no, that mine!'

'Do you want it?' Marly asked.

'Yeth, it mine, Marly. That one miiiine!' Juny pleaded, bunching up her cheeks.

Marly liked it when Juny screeched, all whistly and weak like a bush mouse in a kitchen trap. She thought about Juny touching her special things and somehow, when she thought of the nibbles on her rubber, that noise was good to hear. It joined Marly up inside, a trailer slotting onto a tow-bar, *thunk*. She held Juny's juicy stem up higher, cackling.

Juny jumped up, yelling at Marly now. 'It my-my-mine!'

Marly shoved her back enough to clear a space while she got to her feet. Juny was quick, but Marly was bigger and stronger. Once on her feet, she put one hand on Juny's forehead while the younger girl pushed and fought to get what was hers. Marly giggled and waved the blade of grass a flag in a parade. Juny keened. The girls struggled against each other in a cross-hatched patch of sunlight under a ratty Cocos palm.

'Girls, shut it!' Da half-turned to the backyard.

'Yeah, Juny, shut it!' mimicked Marly.

'Da, Marly got my th-th-thing!' Juny cried.

'I mean it, girls. Ma's gone to work.' Da leaned out over the railing, his face all pale and skinny and twisted up, instead of big and round when Ma got his medicine right. 'Shut the hell up, both of you.'

'Okay, Da,' Marly said, passing Juny her grass.

Juny grinned at her. 'Thank you, Marly.'

She was such a pushover. Marly spat out her own stem onto the dirt, and leaned in close. 'Come on,' she whispered, 'I'll show you the best grass. It's yum!'

'Where ith it?'

'Down by the pod tree.'

'But that not thafe.'

Marly grabbed her hand, and pulled her out past where the

dirt patch gave way to dandelions and asparagus fern. 'It's okay, dummy. All the pods have dropped by now.'

A deep loom of trunks—slender, thick, twisted, straight, firm, rotting—rose all around them. The girls wove through the shade, over hillocks and along little ditches bumpy with tangled roots. Eventually, they reached a sunny patch again. A near perfect circle of tall, skinny trunks rose up and up, so high above their heads it hurt their necks to see the tops. A few dark shapes still nestled among the broad leaves on spreading branches. The loose earth below was pocked with the black-bean pods, each one a torpedo half-buried in the ground.

Juny put her hand around one, then both hands, and pulled it free, dusting off the dirt. 'It tho *heavy*.'

'If one of them hit ya, your brain'd be rice puddin'.' Marly repeated their Da's frequent warning. 'Come on, it's in here.'

Juny strained right back to check nothing was moving up in the treetops, then followed Marly towards the hump that rose in the middle of the trees. The little grove bristled silver and lime with grass as tall as Ma.

'Thnakey?'

'Maybe.' Marly stamped the dirt with her feet and clapped her hands.

Juny threw her pod into the clump of grass and watched the resulting riffles closely. Then she laughed and joined in. 'Go way thnakies, go way thnakies.' Stamp, stamp, clappity-clap.

'This it is, then. This is the best grass.'

Juny's eyes shone in the dappled sun. 'It giant. And there tho much of it.'

'Yes, lots and lots. You go first, now. Like I showed you.'

Juny stepped closer and looked over the tall clump carefully. She spied a long, thick blade within easy reach, and put her hand out.

'Remember, hold it hard and pull it firm. Better use both hands.'

Ten pudgy fingers closed around the blade. She flicked a glance at Marly, as if surprised by the feel of this new wonder. 'It futhy.'

'Yep, it's shiny on the top and fuzzy on the bottom, see?' Marly placed her thumbnail on the top of a shorter blade, bending it over slowly to show Juny both sides, then lifting her thumb off quickly so the grass flashed back up tall, swaying. 'Now, pull!'

Juny scrunched up her nose with determination and jerked her pink fists. Her mouth dropped in shock. She yelped in pain, pulled her hands back and opened her fingers. In her palm lay shreds of the razor grass across two long slashes adorned with red pearls. 'Oweeoweeoweeow!'

'Shut it, crybaby.' Marly stepped back, tilting her head to one side, the blunt ends of her page-girl home-cut hitting the tip of her left shoulder. She watched the pearls form a necklace of blood draped across her sister's hands as Juny hopped and yowled and shook them about.

Marly waited.

Juny's round mouth suddenly went silent; a scream with the sound turned right down. Her eyes popped. She held up her hands in front of her face, then turned them to Marly. Marly leaned forward to check the welts of pin-hair prickles embedded all over Juny's palms, between her fingers, up her wrists.

'It burny burny b-b-burning!'

'Maybe now you'll remember now, hey?' She leaned in close to Juny's tearstained face. 'Stay away from my special things.'

She turned and marched through the bush, taking long strides over hummocks and roots, sure-footed and sturdy. She went all the way back to her patch of dirt in the sun, centred herself between the two grey fingerpaint rainbows bracketing her favourite spot, and settled down cross-legged. She placed her hands flat on the dirt either side of her knees and stared at the scrubby line marking the start of their dark forest.

Minutes later, Juny emerged from the bush, her face splotched black and purple as she desperately sucked at the rash all over her forearms. She traced a wide berth around Marly, heading under the deck to press her body against one of the crumbling concrete poles that held up the house. She sniffled and moaned, snot frothing out of her nose in bubbles that grew big and small, big and small.

Marly glanced up to where her parents had been. She thought that was the top of Da's head she could see, his face slumped over his checked shirt as he balanced, unmoving, in his favourite deck chair. His long legs were two thick, shadowy stripes blocking the slits of light that shone through gaps in the deck floor.

Marly's arms sailed in slow arcs through the silky dust. The rhythm matched her pulse. As she stretched a little further and wider with each long swipe, her fingertips began to tingle.

Brisbane, Queensland, 2010.

*Four hours, four hours, four hours of sleep. Eight hours, eight hours, eight hours of work. Gaming and shower and dinner and gaming.*

Andy was planning his next KorSpace session. In KorSpace, he was GrinreepR, the high-ranked Commander of a tight posse who only knew each other online. But KorSpace forged loyal bonds, and Andy was determined to take them all to the top of the ladder. His new mod pack took six sessions to build. Worth it. Now he could spawn clutches of grinions, and put them to work building a fortress off the Grind, near where his posse had their base.

A blade of aluminium carved into his thoughts. He glanced down. His foot. Pale, with a few soft red curls on the big toe knuckle. He lifted it, and the pain stopped. Placed it back down. Pain.

*Move my foot.*

Andy stretched his thin leg out over the shower trim and stepped into the weak, tepid stream. No, not yet. He curved his torso back and away, just a big lanky S in the middle of a shabby suburban bathroom. As he adjusted the hot tap, a scraping noise growled under his feet. The pipes? The sliding door?

He idled his gaze around the bathroom. Nothing.

Grinions! His posse would decimate the opposition and be back off the Grind before anyone knew what hit them.

Water thrummed in his palm, hypnotic. Waves of it falling in front of his eyes, creating a 4D hologram of infinite fascination; length, width, height, time.

*Four hours, four hours, four hours of sleep. Eight hours, eight hours, eight hours of work. Gaming and dinner and gaming...*

How long before he was snapped back to earth again? A small, warm hand pressed into the curve of his lower back. His coccyx nerves triangulated, spiking out an alarm that netted his whole system. 'What the fuck?'

But that was not right, not the right thing to do. In that situation, with his fiancée—yes, fiancée—making a surprise visit, making contact, he had to remember it was like teacher asking a question, and think before he spoke.

'Is that how you say help to me?' Her lips on his ear.

He answered with a movement from his hips, pushing gently back into her touch. Her fingers flexed, lifting and curving as those painted nails tattooed five tiny smiles on the freckled canvas of his hind parts.

'Why haven't you answered my calls?' Her voice was heavy as mercury. 'You've been glued to that fucking computer again, haven't you?'

Confusion formed ice cubes in his gullet.

'You been ignoring me again? You *promised* this time you'd answer—' *squeeze* '—your damn—' *squeeze* '—phone.'

'I was just getting ready for—'.

Something soft but hard caught him behind the knees. Andy fell like a magician's cloak, velvet swift.

A flash of strong thighs. Laughter bouncing off the tiles. His cheek pressed against cold tile.

'Marlene?' The shape of her name on his thin lips; no sound.


Another downpour drummed across the expanse of corrugated roof covering the single-storey mall. Marlene leaned one bulky thigh into the top step of the ladder, leaving her other foot planted on the bottom rung. She could reach all the way from the middle to the top shelves this way, even the one where they stored overflow stock that wouldn't fit on display. The ladder rattled alarmingly every time she repositioned her frame, reaching left or right, up or down as she filled, moved, rotated and checked tins, packets, boxes and bags of endless goods.

It was the kitchen aisle tonight. She balanced a plastic spatula in one hand, reading the name from the top of the plastic packet. In all her twenty-some years, she'd never used one. She liked its name though. *Spat-u-la.* On impulse she gave a couple of explorative whacks against the ladder. Nice. Then one on her own bum. A loud, satisfying slap shot through the thrum of rain.

*Thwack.*

Marlene smirked and hung it on the row next to its flat-headed brothers. So many kitchen tools arrayed like weapons, and all those women never thinking to use them any way but as intended.

Women were suckers.

The thick polyester polo top, white with a red and green emblem, itched against her chest. She'd been so busy getting Andy organised for the night—a spike of shame at him ignoring here again, flushed away with the pleasure of remembering him prone on the bathroom floor—she'd forgotten to wear her long-sleeved tee underneath. It was too cold in here, especially near the freezer section, only one aisle over. She pulled her hoodie tight around her hips, relying on touch to find the interlock, closing the zip in a series of rough tugs.

Occasionally, Marlene would hear the other two night-fillers working together down in the canned goods aisle, muttering dates and product codes. Why was she here working alone, lugging stuff up and down the ladder, when they had four hands to bucket-line tins around? She was bigger and stronger than anyone else on staff, but it wasn't fair, expecting her to do it all on her own.

'I'm freezing,' one of them complained: Tayla, the giggly school-leaver who could sour Marlene's mood just by showing up.

'Keeps the food fresh.' Hugo was the only permanent on the floor, and had been in the job for longer than any of them, nearly three years—just a few months more than Marlene, even though she'd never made it past being a casual. 'Keeps us awake. And working.'

A clatter of cans hit the ground; an exasperated grunt, a nervous half-laugh.

'Sorry, Mr Koroma.'

Marlene ignored them. She'd nearly finished this pallet but if she took it slow, she could make it last to break time. She checked the fake-but-pretty gold watch her parents gave her for her last birthday, almost oblivious to the rash-red groove its narrow links carved into her wrist. Sure, the birthday card had been in Da's scrambled handwriting, but she recognised her Mother's handiwork: choosing a size too small. Even though Ma was never outright mean to Marlene, she found plenty of other ways to lay the guilt on thick. How hard Ma had worked, how much she did to give her daughters a better life, and how Marlene was just so ungrateful.

Not like Juny, perfect little Juny. Slim and pretty, stayed in school. Got a job as dental assistant, married to a guy with a steady job, saving up to buy their own home. Always doing the right thing, as if she was cooked from different base ingredients to Marly.

Shit, was that the time? Three hours of work under her belt and it was still the middle of the night.

Rubber shoes squeaked as someone approached. A soft wave of heat flushed Marlene's cheeks, but she refused to look around. Soon enough, she could make out a shape next to her; white collar cupping a strong neck. Still, she kept her eyes on her business as she slowly lifted a box of plastic-wrapped wooden spoons up to the overstock shelf.

'Hey, Marlene.'

An electric eel wriggled in her guts. 'Hi, Paulie.'

'Nearly time for a break.'

She half-turned on the ladder, presenting the full width of her pelvis to his pink ear. 'Yep, nearly.'

He kept his eyes on the shelves. 'I got some news you might want to know.'

'Okay.'

'Okay.' He squeaked away. She glanced down at his shoes. Neon yellow high-tops with red piping all around. Gross. But Paulie was her boss, and circling, and kind of buff. So.

Only twenty more minutes. The remembered tang of salty, oily instant noodles set her mouth watering.

She was still fuming about the text from Ma, earlier. The wedding again: the same threats and demands she'd been making every day since Marlene told her parents the big news a week ago. No matter what trip Ma pulled, they wouldn't get to meet Andy until Marlene was good and ready. And never out at Wonglepong. She didn't want Andy to see their manky old house, when his childhood sounded so fancy—mansions and swimming pools and everything, before his parents went bankrupt. It was all out of whack—sure, it was sad about what happened to his parents, but it gave him the upper hand: he didn't have to deal with the whole stress of introducing her to her future in-laws. He was a free agent. She was tied to a history she hated.

Enough. Break time.

The tearoom was in the loading dock; just a sink and a kettle on a temporary shelving unit, shoved into a mouldy corner. She had twenty minutes to eat, pee, and sort out Paulie.

That was how it worked. Every week or so he came by, offered her something, and then took something instead. But Marlene was okay with that. She had a plan.

Marlene always had a plan.

Next morning, Andy stepped off the bus and turned to watch it go, worried he might have left something important behind. As he gazed over the heads of disembarking passengers, a stranger's umbrella scraped across his ankle-bone. Another's elbow caught him in the ribs. Confused, he stepped out of the commuter flow, putting a gentle palm to his right cheek. The painkillers were only helping a little. He checked his pockets. Wallet, phone, security pass.

*Oll korrect, all clear, okay to proceed.*

He liked Tech Park. Its smooth *cul de sac* grace welcomed him, combed the burrs from his thoughts. AmaSecure occupied a ground floor unit deep in the heart of the Park, a fifteen-minute walk from the bus stop. Even at eight in the morning, Andy was sweating in his cheap white business shirt. Wet through, it would turn translucent, revealing pale armpit shadows and sinewy biceps. He only knew because Marlene had pointed it out to him once, the day they were engaged, the look on her face like when she picked green capsicum off her Meatlovers.

He needed her more than he feared her.

Head bowed, he charged up the seven tiled steps and through the sliding doors, ignored the polished receptionist and swiped his way into the workstation area behind.

Sahil didn't look up when Andy took his place beside him at their shared workstation. Instead, Sahil nodded once at the screen before his deft fingers hit the keyboard running; logging on, downloading the day's project brief and opening the tasklist. Sahil was scheduled as lead programmer until ten-thirty, Andy perched on his shoulder to watch each stroke. Then a short break, review, and swap. Repeat.

The JavaScript flowed like Tetris bricks, and it was nearly half an hour before Andy had cause to open his mouth.

'Check that. You need to fix the bound on that loop.'

Sahil argued the point. Sahil always argued the point. Andy never cared. He fixated on the corrupt point of code that would compromise the integrity of weekly customer reports. Folding the latest chip authentication upgrade into their custom security package was tricky. Andy itched for his turn at the keyboard, but until then, he would worry every stroke like a terrier on a tennis ball.

Break time. Sahil checked a final item on the tasklist and logged off. The programming pair at the next workstation was just returning from the staffroom with mugs of coffee: a chatty woman and a new Da who always looked rumpled. Last week, a mad-keen cyclist had paired with her, hanging his sweaty helmet on the corner of the cubicle wall he shared with Andy. But the cyclist had churned without notice. Contract programmers were in high demand, but completely disposable. Easy come, easy go.

The pair stood in the aisle, exchanged a few sentences about the weather forecast for next weekend—talking, laughing—then got seated and settled down to their next task. Andy studied them carefully out the side of his glasses.

He mentally loaded his pre-prepared break conversation opener about the weather, but instead Sahil pushed past the back of Andy's swivel chair to get into the corridor. Andy found himself spun to face the far-side wall. By the time he righted his orientation, Sahil's back was retreating in the direction of the toilets, split diagonally by the black strap of the messenger bag that never left his side.

Andy closed his mouth, turned one full revolution on the chair, looked carefully at every corner of the office, then checked the clock. Studied his shoes a moment. Black walkers with a Velcro buckle.

Silent, just like him.


Marlene leaned against the step ladder, tired, hanging out for the end of her shift. Her phone pinged.

Ma: da needs new medicine come now

Marlene: i'm busy ask juny.

Ma: junette working

Marlene: you shd learn to drive.

Ma: da drive again soon

Marlene: no ma he won't. da won't drive again ever

Ma: what would you know

Marlene: ok I'll come over after work.

Marlene took a big swig of sweet iced tea from a litre bottle and smiled. She'd been wanting some time for a private chat with Da anyway—she'd managed to swing it *and* make Ma think she was doing her a favour. Win-win.

Andy leaned on the counter, grateful for the aircon-cooled laminate against his forearms. He pressed into it, trying to clear his boggled mind; to think and talk at the same time.

'Dale Lewis.' The Processing Officer narrowed his eyes. 'Please stand back.'

'Hey? Oh, right.' Andy stood up straight, and pointed to the photocopied document on the top of the pile. 'My fiancée is Australian. That's her passport.'

'Marlene Kwan Hatchier, born POM 1987—Citizenship by Descent.' The clerk skimmed through the stack of photocopies, each one signed by a Justice of the Peace. 'Father, Australian. Mother, Chinese. Hmm.'

Andy knew all that and couldn't understand why the clerk was reciting this information aloud. What else did they need from him? He waited for a clear sign. He'd tried to avoid this very situation—having to communicate, under duress, with a live human. He'd read every website on the subject, filled out the application, gathered all the documents, tried to submit by courier. But there were too many details—the thread from Australian residency through Marlene to him was tangled and tenuous.

'I'm afraid that your engagement does not qualify you for Partner status. And since the relationship has only pre-existed for…' Paper shuffling.

'Five months,' supplied Andy.

The clerk looked up, wordless, and went back to riffling the stack. Found the document he was searching for and peered at it carefully. 'Five months.'

'Yes.'

'You need a pre-existing relationship of twelve months to qualify.'

'We're practically living together, so I'm just starting the application now. That way, it's processed and ready by the time—'

'It doesn't work that way. You have to qualify first, before you apply. Otherwise, how do we know you won't separate before the waiting period is up?'

'But we're engaged.'

'Engagement doesn't automatically qualify you, sir. You need the requisite pre-existing relationship or a marriage certificate.'

Andy slumped into his shoes, exhausted. Usually, he survived well on four hours sleep, but he'd spent most of the night on the bathmat. He'd left work early to get to the immigration service before closing and raced to catch the connecting bus. His cheekbone throbbed. He couldn't think.

'Our wedding will be very soon.'

'What date?'

'Soon.' Andy leaned forward, earnest. 'As soon as my fiancée and her family decide, ah, well, decide the details.'

'And you are currently in Australia on a tourist visa?'

'No!' Andy was no visitor. He, whose own limitations kept him prisoner in his hometown for nineteen years, had finally broken free. There was literally no home for him to go back to in Mansfield, Ohio. The image of his sister plastered itself across his vision. Thin as wheat, not managing a smile, not even for him. Behind her, a dark shadow in the shape of his mother.

He blinked rapidly, in shock, fighting to get back into his body. 'Sorry, what did you say?'

'What is your current visa status for your stay in Australia please, sir?' The clerk had stopped riffling. He was getting that look on his face like shopkeepers do when kids browsed the candy racks with their school bags still on. 'Do you have a current visa?'

'My work visa. Remember? This one,' Andy leaned over the counter to show him the form they had looked at when the interview began.

'Stand back, sir.'

Tendrils of anxiety wrapped around Andy's windpipe. He

took a slow breath in through his nose. He must not lose it. Leaning back on his heels, he put the clerk out of reach.

'Okay, here we are.' The clerk perused the clipped bundle of current visa papers, pausing at Andy's list of qualifications. 'IT and IST? Is that a typo?'

'Information Technology is computers. IST is computer-operated machinery.'

'North Central State?' The clerk looked up at Andy's face, his tone both patronising and curious. 'You're a bit young to have a double degree, aren't you?'

Andy's pulse hammered in his temples. 'I was good at math so I, um, got through it early. Quicker. And it's not a double degree—IST is only an Associate.' The cheapest course possible to insert himself into the Ohio State system. Once he was in, he could tweak his academic record to say whatever he wanted, so now it said what he needed it to say. He knew more about coding than they could ever have taught him at State anyway.

'Okay, that's all fine as far as your current visa goes. Now,' the clerk checked the time, 'look. We close in a few minutes, and there's really nothing we can do with this application in your current circumstances.'

'But I'm halfway through a one-year visa. I don't have seven months left here to qualify for a pre-existing relationship, only six. I'm marrying an Australian.' Andy's voice climbed, thin and desperate, into his sinus cavity. 'It's just one-month. What's the difference?'

'One month is one month.' The clerk shrugged and gave his first smile of the interview. 'Come back and try again if you get married.'


A cool breeze tickled the sweat around Marlene's hairline, carrying the musty tang of distant burn-offs. She pushed her Da over a rough path through the barbecue tables out the back of Saint Bernard's pub, perched high on the northern ridge of Tamborine Mountain.

'Fucking hell, darling.' Terry's voice was deep as a cave, a broken beast hiding inside. 'Take it easy on your old man.'

'No point coming here if we don't get the view.' Her hands slipped on the grip of the wheelchair, a cheap-arse one they walked out from the hospital last year, since he refused to buy himself one. 'You need a better chair, Da.'

'This thing?' He slapped the grey plastic armrest. 'I never use it—only when you or your sister take me out.'

'That's just because me and Juny are the only reason you ever go out.' Marlene jerked the chair in frustration until it lined up with the rough-cut end of the farthest table. 'Ma is too busy all the time to do anything with you.

'Well, your Ma has a lot on her plate. I get around okay, Marls, don't worry.' Terry locked the wheels and Marlene stood behind him, both of them gazing out over the purple mists that smothered green peaks and haze-shadowed valleys as far as you could see; all the way to Brisbane, an hour's drive north.

Marlene plonked down the silver wedge with their table number and dropped her handbag onto the bench. She slid in sideways, pushing the seat further out with the back of her knees, and settled herself down.

She flicked a glance at her Da. His fingers wove slowly in his lap. His wasted shoulder hung forward and down; his grey-blue eyes were bleached to dishwater from decades of pain meds.

'Here you go!' An overly cheerful waitress served two frosted glasses of beer. 'Top spot you've got here, nice and cool.'

'Yes, darling.' Terry swivelled his head to smile. 'Lovely, thanks.'

The waitress reached for the table number. 'Anything else coming?'

'Fish 'n' chips,' growled Marlene.

She swept her camel lashes over Marlene's bulk, gave a smub smile, and dropped her arm. 'Okay then.'

'Cheers.' Da held up his glass, tipped it carefully towards his daughter. 'And how's your fella going?'

'Good. At work today.'

'Computers, isn't it?'

'That's right, Da.'

He slunk a look up at her from under his lids. 'Your Ma's wondering when do we get to see him.'

'Why, so she can tell me how bad he is?'

'Hang on, Marly. You've gone and got engaged, after just a couple of months, and we still haven't had a chance to meet him.' He scratched his beard with worry. 'I know your Ma can be tough on you, but all she wants is—'

'I know what she wants.' Marlene's fingertips were wet from the glass. She traced them around the bright gold ring on her fourth finger. It was shaped in an elongated M, like a kid's drawing of a bird in flight. 'Da, we're going to need some help with the wedding. We've been trying to save, but I don't get regular shifts, and by the time we've paid for rent and food and petrol and everything, there just isn't enough.'

'It's my job to do it, darling—you shouldn't have to ask. I'm your Da.' Terry sighed, his left shoulder slumping to match his right. 'I've always said I'd pay for the whole thing. Not just your wedding—enough to set you up in life, get you started.'

Marlene relaxed as her plan clicked into place. 'I knew you'd come through. Thanks, Da.' She'd dreamed of this moment: her long-promised nest egg. This wedding money would be Marlene's chance to get ahead. She hated that she never had enough money, hated that her own wage didn't even cover the very basics, hated the rattling shit-box Datsun Andy let her use. Even though it was sweet of him, every time it got stuck in second gear, it reminded her that she was worthless in the eyes of the world.

Andy, as great as he was with computers, was completely backward about anything official—overcome with shyness at any mention of shared bank statements or rental agreements. Once they were married, she'd make Andy get that joint account. But a little pile in her own private account—from her own Da, so she was entitled—wouldn't go astray.

Her heart thudded against her breastbone with excitement. It wasn't that she was obsessed with having nice stuff, like Juny was—it was more about feeling safe and steady, like she was in a sleek yacht with a deep rudder, instead of forever clinging to a leaky fucking raft that went over every time the wind changed.

Marlene noticed Da was moaning quietly, his eyes closed, the skin around them crinkled and grey. 'You hurting, Da?' She reached in her bag for his new tablets, but he spoke before she popped the lid.

'I should pay for the wedding, but I can't. I'm so sorry, darling.'

'What?' Marlene sat still as cursed stone.

The waitress bounced up with two full plates. Marlene's scowl killed the chatter before it left her lips—she served wordlessly and bustled away.

'There's nothing—we've got nothing left, Marls.' A tear leaked down a wrinkle towards his ear. 'You know I'd do anything for you. But we met with the bank last week, and they won't help us out again. We're struggling just to hold on to the house.'

'But you've got money set aside—I know you do. Junette told me about it.' Furious, powerless, Marlene balled her fists around the knife and fork.

'I'm sorry, love, but it's gone. Medical bills. Rates. Everything. It all adds up.'

'But—your insurance, your pension? You paid for Junette's wedding last year. You guys have plenty!' A rift opened in Marlene's chest, threatening to suck her down once and for all. She recognised it: the gaping hole that she somehow knew she got from her Da, that he and Ma'd been trying to paper over with fake promises her whole life.

She looked at her father and saw a different man. He'd always been so huge—tender or mean by measure of his meds— but always a giant of a man. The pictures of him in full leathers, mounted on a massive Duke. The size of his fist when she didn't want to go to preschool, wrapping twice around her upper arm.

Now, she saw that he was weak: a trembling ghost of manhood, dribbling apologies into the lap of a crappy stolen wheelchair. Marlene grasped the reality of her situation and her mind turned, hard and quick. If he was weak, that meant she was stronger. There must be some way she could play the situation; jump her pawn all the way to the end of the board and win the crown.

But it would take some thought.

'Don't worry about it.' She cut off his excuses. 'We'll sort something out. Eat your fish.' Marlene shoved a forkful of chips in her mouth and reached for the tomato sauce, squeezing a rude flood of scarlet across everything on her plate.


Marlene sought a cool patch, stretching her toes over onto what had become Andy's side of the bed when she stayed over. A faded field of tiny yellow and pink flowers swayed over her —handed down from Ma and on permanent loan to Andy. Beneath, her calves felt clogged as damp soil. She flicked off the sheet and hefted her bum further over onto the vacant space.

She sucked her pointer finger. 'Hey, come to bed!' Each nipple shone in turn, glossed with spit.

A long silence followed, broken by occasional spurts of keyboard clacking. Had he heard her? Was he thinking about his answer? She could never tell—he was so slow, it was like waiting for a broken light to go green.

Both hands at work now, she paused, frustration prickling her ready flesh. 'You hear me?'

'Yes, I just—' Tappity tap tap.

'Well?' Her veins tightened. She hated it when he made her ask twice.

'I just have to finish building this—'.

'But I'm ready now. Come to bed.'

Pause. 'Okay.' She heard him start his nightly procedures: clickety-click, tap, snap, scrape. Three careful clinks in the kitchen to rinse and drain his cup. To the bathroom: slosh, splash, scrub.

She rested a middle finger at the top of her slick vee and rasped a thumbnail over her regrowth. 'Come on, hurry up.'

He reached the bedroom doorway, saw her, and stopped.

Confusion rippled across his damp brow. 'Oh-oh. Left side, right side. Ha. Okay. Um, light off?'

She waggled her hips deeper into the groove on his side of the bed, savouring this exquisite morsel of triumph. 'Light on.'

He slid off the jail-blue jeans he wore every single night, winter or summer, and glanced over at her questioningly. Usually, he would drape them over the back of the chair that doubled as his bedside table, but since Marlene was on his side of the bed, he seemed unsure as to whether he had lost all rights to that part of her room, and if so, where he should put his jeans.

She softened her voice. 'Just throw them on the floor and get in, jeez.'

'Okay.'

As soon as his weight hit the bed she rolled away and shoved her bum into him until he turned to cradle it with his soft, narrow crotch. She reached back and gripped his forearms then rolled away, pulling him with her so that she ended up facedown with the full length of his frame resting along her back, his body a thin pale line down her spine, his cock prone between her cheeks.

'Did you get it sorted?'

'They say I can't get residency yet.'

'What?' She dug her fingers into his wrists. 'Didn't you tell them we're engaged?'

'Yes, but they said that's not enough. They said we have to be married.' His heartbeat pressed against her back, tapping quick and hard as a prospector's hammer.

'Oh for fuck's sake, that's what engaged means, right? Getting married! What do they think, we can just pull the wedding money out of our arse?'

'Have you spoken to your Da yet?'

'Yeah. No fucking help, as per usual. But I'll handle it. I'm getting a proper wedding, not some visa rush-job.'

'But what about... I mean, of course. You just tell me what you need me to do.'

'All you have to do is get your residency stuff sorted. I don't want to end up a mail-order widow or some shit. Now look, I've been thinking. About Paulie's news, you know? It might mean we can get married a bit sooner.' She smiled, teeth pressed into the pillowcase, remembering Paulie's fingers coiled tight in her hair. 'Since he's leaving the shop.'

'You never said how come.'

'He's saved up enough for his big trip.'

'Did he say where he's going?'

'Nowhere—all over. Starting in Bangkok.'

'So, he's not coming back?'

'Nope, not for ages.'

Andy squeezed air around his soft palate; his thinking noise. He cock flickered to life in her crack. 'Well, I guess his going sure opens up an opportunity. All those savings.'

'I know, right?' Her hands tingled with adrenalin; she rubbed them against the pilled sheets. 'But what do you reckon—has it been long enough since the last one? Could we get away with it again?'

'Let's see what we can find out. Maybe you could invite him over—do you reckon he'd come?'

Marlene smirked. 'Oh, yeah, he'd come if I asked.'

Andy slowly grinding against her. 'Plus, if you wanted, you could probably even get his job.'

'Yeah, I could.' Her tailbone lifted, thighs opening, an invitation for his hips to curl down and around her behind, until his cock dropped into place. She reached one hand underneath herself to tug him into position,. She tilted her hips up and back, humming his name high and soft as they rocked together.

*An-an-an-deeeee.*

He'd dropped into her hands like coins from a poker machine, this nobody from nowheresville. For the first time in as long as she could remember, Marlene felt in control.

II.

The snake slid forward, tongue tasting the night air for skinks. A large shape crouched in the corner of the crawlspace, staining the dark shadows around it foul and sweet. The snake reared and froze, waiting. The shape's narrow end was pressed to the floorboards above; its thick middle prone on the dirt. The snake limboed to one side and out between the warped battens. Leaf litter crackled in the stillness.

The shape shifted slightly in response, making sure never to stray from the tiny hole, drilled through the pinewood floor.

Marlene should be leaving for work. Next ad break, for sure. Her phone buzzed.

Ma: why you upset da

Marlene: you mean he upset me.

Ma: you know he not well

Ma: and feel really bad about it all

Marlene: >:[

Ma: I feel bad too.

*Excuse me, did her mother just apologise to her? Get the fuck out of here!*

> Marlene: :(:(:(

> Ma: you want to come for bbq this sunday
> bring andy

> Marlene: I hate u ur ruining my life

> Ma: junette and steve bring fresh crabs

Marlene popped her lips. Ma's chili crab was probably the best thing about her. She winced and tossed her phone onto the couch beside her. Lay back for a moment, scanning internally. *There.* Gassy and tender. She pushed down the elasticated waistband on her denim skirt and rubbed her belly, wondering if a fizzy drink would help. She would nick one from the storeroom at work.

Ma could wait.

Even Paulie looked good in the pale fluoro light of the tearoom. He'd rolled up the sleeves on his black business shirt so they tucked in perfectly under his biceps.

'What will you get up to in Thailand?' Marlene pressed her chin to her shoulder and checked. All clear. Still turned away, she leaned in until her left breast pressed against him. 'All sorts of trouble, I guess.'

His hand slid up her polo shirt, squeezing until she opened her mouth to protest, then releasing and caressing, pressing upwards. 'I'll get around and see all kinds of stuff, Marlene. I heard about this river you can ride,' his palm found her flat disc of breast meat, and he puffed a hot breath into her ear, 'on a tyre tube.' His thumb reached for her dimpled ellipse and circled. 'You start way up in Laos. You can order fancy drinks from peasants on jetties along the sides. You ride it all the way,' he flicked and pinched, 'to Burma.'

A door hissed behind them. Footsteps approached. Marlene

drew back slowly. Paulie's hand ran down her torso all the way to her undercarriage. He gave her a squeeze then released, locking her into some serious eye contact. She kept her face blank as an empty shelf.

Hugo Koroma came in, saw the two of them standing there, and dropped his eyelids a fraction. He walked over and took a plastic cup from the bench, carefully examining the circular ghost of dust underneath. As he rinsed and drank, Marlene spoke to Paulie, loud enough for Hugo to hear.

'Hey, you want to come to over for dinner sometime? You can meet my fiancé. Say goodbye and that.' *Fuck you, Hugo. I'm getting this job, and more.*

'Sure, sure. You and Andy? That's great. I leave pretty soon, but just let me know when.' His lips twitched in a smile just wide enough to show blunt incisors. 'You better get back to work.'

'Yeah. See ya.' Marlene took her time leaving, enjoying the heft and sway of her hips, heels sliding sideways off her non-regulation sandals with every step.


Eight acres in Wonglepong, overgrown with gorgeous, pest-riddled bush: balloon vines and tortured willows and noxious camphor laurels. It had seemed a slice of PNG right here in South-East Queensland, lush with serenity, when they bought it for a song back in the late eighties. Terry had hoped it would help Dionne settle. Instead, it made everything worse: each hardship grew more intense, echoing against the khaki folds of nearby Mount Misery, no one to buffer them from their problems. Or from themselves.

Twenty-odd years of neglect malformed the idyllic cottage into a fairy tale nightmare, hard evidence of his failings of heart and limb. The yard was littered with the corpses of abandoned repair jobs: broken refrigerators and motorcycle bones.

He leaned his bum on the railing as his small family scraped their chairs across faded wooden decking. The new bloke, Andy, was hard to read. Terry's meds bred dark ghosts across his sight and stripped his other senses bare. He lived bunkered in a desert storm and most days it was too much effort to care. But today, he had a job to do, one of his last fatherly duties before he simply lay down and surrendered to the predictable maelstrom of his agonies.

He had to get a handle on Andy.

He squinted, trying to bring his prospective son-in-law out of the bleached summer shadows. Orange-red hair, pale skin, long and thin. Wordless and unsmiling and awkwardly put together. Not what he expected at all, after Marlene's serial interest in nuggety little Hitlers.

'Marlene, come take out the bread,' Dionne called from the kitchen. 'And make sure everyone has drinks.'

'Why me?' Marlene groaned and pushed back her chair. She pulled Andy's hand so that he rose with her. 'May as well give you the tour while we're here.' They disappeared down the narrow hall to the bedrooms.

Steve—Junette's fella—reached over to the esky, pulling out a couple of beers and letting the lid fall shut. He passed one to Terry. 'Smells alright, hey?' He glanced towards the kitchen.

Terry nodded. The warm afternoon air was layered with flavour: chili and palm sugar, soy and prawn heads. 'Juny and Dionne are a crack team.' He gripped the bottle-top between his thighs and twisted. Took a sip. 'So, you met this Andy before?'

'Nah.' Steve drank, deep chugs that formed whale spouts in the upturned bottle.

Terry watched Steve's beer disappear, envious. He trickled another spoonful down his own permanently stricken gullet. 'What's his story?'

'He's a Yank. Juny says he works in computer security.'

'What's that when it's at home?'

Steve shrugged. 'I think, like, you pay his company to make sure no one rips off your credit card when you're buying stuff online.'

They stared blankly at each other for a moment.

'But, what does he actually, you know, do?'

'I'm not sure. It's probably like insurance, or a security alarm.

Like if someone else uses your card somewhere, his company tracks it.'

Terry's mind swirled around that one for a minute. 'They can tell where you are when you're on the computer?'

'Sure. That, plus your phone and whatever else—bloody government knows everything you do, nowadays.'

'Then what do we need that computer security whatever insurance for?'

'Ah shit, I don't know, Terry.' Steve laughed, a low bark from his muscled gut. 'I make fucking tinnies for a living.'

Terry chuffed through his nose, relieved to be on familiar ground. 'Yeah, and where's mine, mate? I'm still waiting.'

'Ha! Get your boat licence, old man, and we'll talk.'

'Licences for everything, insurance for everything, bloody hell.' He dropped his chin. 'All this shit—it does, it makes me feel like an old man.'

Dionne emerged holding a steaming wok of dismantled crabs swimming in tiny rings of red and green. 'Where is the bread?' She lowered the wok down on the table and turned back inside. 'Marlene! The bread?'

'Yeah, yeah, coming.' Marlene emerged from the hall, smoothing her side-parted fringe behind one ear. Terry watched as she grabbed two loaves of spongy white bread, squeezing them appreciatively. 'Where's the marge?'

'Ma says no marge.' Junette balanced a stack of plates on her forearm.

Marlene groaned and pushed past Junette to wrench open the fridge door. She grabbed the yellow plastic container and came out to the deck, dumping a loaf and the margarine on the table, throwing the other loaf to Steve. 'Think quick!'

Steve batted it away easily, redirecting the loaf onto the table, steering clear of the bottles and glasses. 'Where's your bloke?'

'In the loo, actually.' A wave of annoyance passed over Marlene's brow. 'Give us a beer.'

Andy stepped out onto the deck, flicked his gaze over the now laden table as though cataloguing each new item, and made a beeline for his chair.

Terry cleared his throat. 'Beer, Andy?'

'Do you have a cola?'

'Junette, grab Andy a Coke, love.'

Juny appeared a moment later, holding a can of drink.

'Everybody, sit. Eat while it's hot.' Dionne reached for the biggest claw and cracked the hard shell with two blows from the wrong end of a table knife. She plated it up for Terry, as he tilted his stiff body down into the chair at the head of the table. Everyone followed Dionne's lead, picking out the best pieces on offer, scooping up as much sauce as the slotted spoons would hold.

*Slurp, crack, slurp.* Terry lost himself in the physical work of eating crab one-handed, sucking the meat out with his tongue when he couldn't dislodge it with a fork or finger.

Dionne nudged his elbow, and he moved it out of her way. She nudged it again. He looked up.

Marlene was tackling Andy's crab, showing him how to break the legs at the joints, bending them slowly to pull out the flesh still attached to a sliver of internal cartilage.

Dionne and Terry raised their eyebrows at each other, shared a tentative smile.

Terry turned his attention back to the crab, soaking a soft piece of bread in the gutsy juices. He heard Dionne suddenly catch her breath and looked up to see her frowning. He followed her gaze to Marlene, squirming in her chair, hands smeared with sauce, rubbing her upper arm awkwardly back and forth across her chest.

'What wrong? You do that all day.'

'Nothing. I'm just itchy.'

'Heat rash again?'

'Ma, shut up.'

Dionne flicked her gaze at Terry, but he looked down without giving anything away. He knew his wife wished more of her own grace had passed on to Marlene, but, well, she could lighten up a bit on the girl. Especially in front of the new boyfriend.

'Marlene, we need paper towels.'

'Aw, Ma-a.'

'Now, please.'

Marlene sighed but stood and moved to the kitchen. A cupboard opened, then another. 'Where are they?'

Dionne was already on her feet. 'I show you.' She disappeared into the kitchen, and a series of low hisses and gasps followed.

'What are you doing in there?' Terry asked after a minute. 'Better be quick or we'll eat yours!'

Marlene appeared in the doorway, head down, self-conscious, pulling her shirt-front down and over the top of her skirt. She looked deathly pale. Dionne nudged her out onto the deck.

As she passed behind his chair, Dionne leaned down and hissed in Terry's ear. 'You talk to that new man after lunch.'

Terry looked around in surprise. 'Why?' he mouthed.

'Because your daughter is pregnant,' Dionne whispered back.

'Who's pregnant?' Junette's voice was sharp as a new pencil.

Andy froze with a can of Coke halfway off the table. Steve shoved a ball of bread into his mouth and chewed without closing his lips.

'Marlene?' Junette pressed.

'Ma says I've got the signs.'

'Itchy nips? Far out!' A mean flicker of delight crossed Junette's face before she creased her brow into a frown of concern. 'You better get tested.'

'Pfft, test.' Dionne flicked her fingers sideways with a click. 'You are pregnant. Stupid, stupid girl.'

Marlene sent a fierce look at Andy. 'If I am preggers, we better get organised. Especially if Da reckons he can't help out with the wedding or anything.'

Andy carefully put down his can of drink, keeping his eyes on his lap. 'It's okay. I'll take care of you, Marlene.'

'How?' Dionne demanded. 'You look like a kid.'

'I'm nineteen, ma'am.'

'Nineteen! A new baby?' Dionne's voice cut across the rough bushland surrounding the deck. 'You don't know—a baby will change everything! A baby is going to need a proper house. You need clothes, furniture. You got to keep a baby *safe*.' She was nearly screaming, tendons standing out above her clavicles.

Terry's solar plexus spasmed as the news sunk in. His daughter, pregnant. A blood-soaked baby Marly in her crib back in Moresby: the image speared through the mists, shredding his breath. He flinched. All he wanted was to set her up in life, make sure she was safe.

But he couldn't even pay for her wedding. Instead, she had to rely on some teetotalling foreigner barely old enough to vote.

'I've still got all my tools. You could get second-hand furniture and we can fix it up nice.' Terry's words sounded thin to his own ears, pathetic. 'Like we used to do, remember? We built that dolly cot together. When you girls were little?'

Marlene's face stayed chalky and vacant.

Andy cleared his throat quietly. 'I guess, well, Marlene can move into my place. Permanently. If she wants to.' He spoke so low, everyone leaned in to hear him. 'And I've got a bit saved up to help with the baby, or whatever.'

Marlene's eyes glinted. She exchanged a meaningful look with her sister. Terry had seen them trade that look a million times. Scheming.

Junette turned to Andy with new regard. 'Really? That's cool. Can you pay for the wedding, too?'

Terry picked up his beer and sculled until he choked, forcing the bitter liquid down past his rising gorge.


Andy adjusted the bones of his bare backside on the computer stool. He was having trouble settling in this session. A strange sensation crawled up his spine. He glanced around the empty lounge room. Marlene had left for the shops half an hour ago, complaining about his empty fridge.

His cheeks started to burn, self-conscious for no reason. His reached for his jeans, folded over the back of his chair, and tugged them up his legs, jumping up to fasten the fly. He never expected visitors—apart from Marlene, no one even knew where he lived. Pants on, he sat down and entered the world of KorSpace.

As GrinreepR, he rode a rough beast cobbled together from dismembered parts left behind after a surprise attack. His posse members, DatPwns and lunajonny, sent frantic chatter his way, messages popping up in the bottom left corner of the screen. They'd been robbed, completely griefed, and were all heading for the grey mist that would reload them back onto the Grind.

Passionless fury flashed a torch across Andy's thoughts. The player known as Achachak had disrupted his careful strategy, stealing a month's worth of hoarded game credit: kred. On his second screen—just a laptop so no good for gaming, but with plenty of grunt for sidebar tasks—Andy started a deep web search, trawling for connections. It would take time, but he would find the clue that led him to the human behind the avatar Achachak, and then analyse their online usage patterns. Knowledge is power.

Meanwhile, Andy kept working the WASD with his left hand, riding the beast hard, and broke into some chat.

Clutches of grinions unfurled and set to work.

> GrinreepR: lets meet at chubers

> DatPwns: can't I lost my status

> lunajonny: yeh but grinreepr has big stash there right?

> GrinreepR: big enough to get achachak

> DatPwns: ok meet you outside

lunajonny and DatPwns tore ahead on their fully formed mounts.

Andy spent another half an hour organising his inventory and researching a new game plan. A thin smile stretched his lips as he logged off, mind ticking over methodically. He had pieced together enough of Achachak's history to know he was up against an experienced contender.

But maybe Achachak was a godsend. If Andy worked it right, he could fold this bold interloper into his plans—an ally? a mark?—and amplify them, taking things to a grander scale, bagging a greater haul.

As he cleaned his glass and headed for the bathroom, the floorboards rapped in a weird rippling rhythm, barely audible. Andy wasn't used to wooden floorboards—all those joints and knots and nails. Nor was he used to the abundant suburban menagerie in his backyard—he knew only jerky-thin feral cats, not growling possums and handspan spiders and fat-bellied birds raining mockery from the telegraph wires.

He stood still for a minute, listening intently to the cricket-chirrup silence. When he moved, the rapping started up again.

Something about this house reminded Andy of the trailer back in Mansfield; small and low-set, but creepy as a labyrinth. His Adam's apple climbed into the back of his throat, and he swallowed it painfully back into place. He lay on the bed fully dressed and dozed until Marlene came back.

Next morning, he noticed they'd run out of milk. He opened the dusty cupboard that served as his pantry, checking for marshmallows and peanuts in the shell—the stuff Marlene usually kept stocked for snacks.

The cupboard was empty.


Marlene usually avoided her family's company like the plague, especially now she'd moved out—Ma could be such a bitch, Da was just so depressing, and Juny was basically a mini-Ma so they nearly always took each other's side. But Ma was copping a taste of her own guilt, now there was the threat of a baby and no family money for the wedding. Now, Ma was constantly inviting Marlene to drop by or come shopping or pick her up and go to Junette's, and Marlene wasn't one to say no to free stuff along with a bit of attention and respect for a change.

Even though, sometimes, Ma would get this funny look on her face when she saw Marlene. Like she wanted to squeeze her until it hurt.

Today, Dionne was neat as ever in tan slacks and a colourful buttoned blouse. She packed snake beans down the side of her canvas shopping trolley, taking care not to crush the green spoon leaves of the bái cài.

Marlene and Junette waited, rolling their eyes at each other.

'Ma, why do we have to come here?' Junette looked around the Darra markets, a ramshackle square bristling with cars parked nose-in to the curb. 'Why can't you just shop in a normal shop?'

'Like mine.'

'Yeah, like where Marly works?'

'Those shops are no good.' Dionne gave her charcoal bouffant a sharp shake. 'The food here is fresh and cheap.'

'You're such a tight-arse.'

'Hey,' Dionne smacked Marlene's arm. 'I feed you all this time —even if we have plenty of money, or no money at all.'

'The food here sucks.' Marlene balanced a bag of salty plums in her hand, before tossing it onto Ma's collection of items on the counter. 'Must have been so great, though, when you and Da got all that money.'

'What money?' Junette's eyes glinted with suspicion.

'You know, when we were little. Ma got all this money one time from some old guy who died, up in PNG.'

'Your Grandfather!' Dionne snapped, then turned her back on the girls, hands moving quickly to pack her items in an cardboard box labelled Sunny Apples. 'Anyway, doesn't matter. That money is all long gone.'

'It was great for a while, though. That Christmas, Junette and I got brand new scooters. Yours had purple tassels out the handlebars. Mine were pink.' She screwed up her nose. *Pink. She'd wanted the purple.* The bright, hungry joy in Da's eyes as he led them under the house to unveil the gift faded quickly, as Marly shredded her sister's pretty tassels.

A thought occurred to Marly. 'Hey, we got any other rich rellos up there that are gonna leave us more piles of dough?'

'Pssh! My family is gone. They didn't like it when we moved to Brisbane after... what happened.' Dionne's eyes drifted away, the way they always did when she mentioned Da's accident.

A heavy stone shifted in Marlene's chest. She swayed, catching the edge of the checkout bench just in time. Fucking pregnancy. Although, it had happened before, that sudden swoon. Plenty of times, before she got pregnant; this sudden shifting of the ground under her feet. Flickering images of her father free-falling down a pitch-dark mineshaft, the sound of screaming. His broken body. Blood everywhere; on Da, on Ma. On Marly herself.

A quick shake of her head: no. The dizziness passed as quickly as it came, leaving a high-pitched buzz in her ears.

'Yeah, that must have been tough, your family turning their back like that.' Junette was giving Ma a sympathetic pat on the shoulder. 'But also, you know, where did all that money go? Weren't you rich in PNG?'

'My family had plenty. We had servants, cars, a boat. My father bought me everything I needed, and then your father came along and took care of me. But then...' Ma neatly restacked the salty plums next to the other heavier items: bulk rice, a giant daikon radish. She gave Junette a rare frown. 'Anyway, no one said either of you have to eat this food. It is for Da and me.'

'Da hates it, too.' Marly kept her face expressionless as she delivered this home truth.

Ma's face was smooth for her fifty-odd years but mapped with coin spots of eczema that migrated around, never completely disappearing. There was a nasty patch starting near her ear. The patch twitched as Marlene stared, making her wonder if it was the itch or her criticism of Ma's cooking that pained her.

'Come on, Marlene, men like good cooking. You need to learn.' Ma's voice had a rare hint of sweetness. 'Maybe I can show you?'

'What, like, you come over to my new place?' Marlene caught her breath. 'Maybe, once I've got everything set up. If you want.'

'Yes, I can teach you. Like, this food—', she swept her hand over the grocery box, '—is best for keeping Da healthy and strong.' She ran her eyes quickly over Marlene's silhouette. 'We can cook, and talk. You can learn about babies. About my births. About what you were like, when you a baby, you and your sister.'

At this unprecedented display of maternal tenderness, Marlene's tough hide softened. Confused, she reached for the salty plums, splitting open the packet and tucking one in her cheek. The familiar tang instantly made her belly weird and crampy.

'Yeah, whatever, Ma.' She grabbed Junette's elbow and headed for the door. 'We'll be in the op shop round the corner, see if there's anything good.'

Dionne dug around in her oversized handbag for her purse. 'Don't buy anything until I come, too—I know Mr Li.'

Marlene dropped Junette's arm as soon as they hit the footpath and spat the sucked plum seed out into the gutter.

'Ergh.' Junette wrinkled up her nose at Marly. 'I'm so boooored. How long is this gonna take?'

'Jeez, it'll only be a few minutes. You're gonna be an aunty. Don't you even care?'

'Sure.' Junette gazed thoughtfully at Marlene's belly. 'What's it feel like?'

'Gross. I'm starving all the time, but I can't hardly eat anything except noodles. And my boobs are so sore. I just want to sleep.'

They stepped into the cluttered second-hand store. Random furniture items stood back-to-back, forming narrow aisles. Drab woollen coats bred dust mites on huddled racks. Marlene examined the layout, choosing the widest pathway to the back of the store, where a faded sign hung from the low ceiling: Babies & Children.

Junette beat her there, popping out from behind a white cupboard with crackled faults across its mirrored sliding door. 'Hey, check this.'

Marlene looked at the woven yellow basket, feeling stupid. 'What's that thing for?'

'Really? You gonna be a mum and you don't even know? It's a bouncer.'

'It's fugly as.' Marlene snatched it off Junette, turning it over and poking her fingers through the crocheted holes. 'How does the baby even fit?'

'Put it here. Like this.' She took the bassinette and lay it on a cracked laminate table, then put her forearm in it and wiggled her fingers. 'See? My hand is the head. Steve's sister in Wollongong had one, but hers isn't knitted.'

'So, it's like a bed?'

'Yeah, but like, during the day, so you don't have to hold the kid the whole time.' She pushed down and then lifted out her arm, setting the bouncer into wild action. 'You just stick it in here and then you get on with whatever you were doing.'

'Shit, you'll break it.' Marlene picked it up and read the sticker, stuck on the curve of the metal base that was shaped like a coat-hanger folded over in half. 'It's only five bucks.'

'You gonna get it?'

'Yeah.' Marlene clamped her teeth. Junette thought she knew more about babies, when Marlene was the pregnant one? Well, fuck her. 'I'm getting it.'


The trunk of the Datsun overflowed with Marlene's op shop bounty: stiff towels, powdery doonas, and semi-broken small appliances. When Andy arrived in her life, he showed up with nothing more than a backpack and a willingness to please. He seemed to know less about homemaking than even she did. The only item of value he owned was his giant-screened computer.

Marlene had never cared about homemaking stuff, either. But there was a baby coming. The weight of history was in her belly, invisible to the world, rocking her foundation. If setting up house was what it took to put her back in charge, then that's what she would do. And she did enjoy the idea of officially making Andy's place her own: a two-bedroom, low-set fibro house set smack in the middle of a dead flat square block, two doors down from a busy bus stop.

'What's that?' Andy eyed a red metal box the size of picnic basket, the latch dented, scarred all over with rusty scratches.

Marlene hauled it out, the weight of it making one arm hang low. 'Da's loaned us his tools. In case we need to fix anything up.' She stepped into a long, narrow tyre-trench that formed one half of the driveway. 'Ma thinks this place is a bit of a dump, I guess.'

'Can I see?'

Marlene dropped the box with a crash and flipped open the lid. Dull drill bits and old screws were tossed randomly into little compartments. She lifted out the top layer to reveal a hammer and a couple of hand tools: a garden saw, a drill with a cracked jam crawl. It all stank of rust.

'Your Da used all these?'

'Yeah, course. He used to. And he showed me a lot of stuff, too. I can, like, hang a shelf, change a bulb, whatever.'

'Really?'

'Yeah.' Marlene picked up the drill. A breeze moved her sweaty fringe. Time stood still. An urge lurched up from deep inside her—an impulse to reach for something crouched just outside of reason. Something to do with her father and her and this new blob in her belly. Something to make sense of this spiralling chasm that linked them together and held them apart.

'Hold out your hand.' Marlene centred the bit in his palm then cranked the handle a quarter turn.

'Ow.' Andy snatched his hand away. For a moment it looked like he might keep raising it. Anger flared in his eyes.

Marlene laughed at him. 'Grab it by the handle.'

'I know how to use a drill, Marlene.' Andy took the worn wooden handle in his left hand and lowered it to the packed ground at his feet. 'I just haven't seen this sort before.'

'Just crank the handle until the drill digs in.' She watched as he worked the drill, creating a small mound of grey dirt. 'See? It's easy.'

Andy tried to pull the drill straight up, but it was trapped.

'Wind it the other way, dickhead.' Marlene turned back to the boot and leaned in, wrapping her arms around as big a load as she could manage. She emerged, her face nearly buried in doona. She glanced at Andy as she passed him: he was cranking the drill into the air in front of his face, hypnotised. She wanted to smack him back to the here and now, but her hands were full. 'Come on. Pack it up, and bring the box, will ya.' She bumped him with her hip, hard.

He flinched and looked up at her, guilty.

'What the hell goes on in that brain of yours, Andy? I can never tell what you're thinking about, or if you're even thinking at all.'

He smirked a little. 'I think about absolutely everything, Marlene. All the time.'

She ignored him and carefully made her way up the five cement steps leading to the tiny porch.

It only took a few loads each, and the car was empty. Marlene stood in the boxy lounge room, trying to decide if she should chuck all the stuff off the faded brown couch, or go and clear the bed. Either way, she had to crash for a while. She was straight off a night shift, with another one ahead of her.

That was the best thing about this baby coming—she wouldn't have to work this shitty job for a while. Plus, if she got the Night Manager job she'd be permanent, and then they'd have to pay her maternity leave or something, she was pretty sure.

Marlene looked around and couldn't see Andy anywhere, so she just yelled, 'We'll have to tidy all this shit up before we can have Paulie over for tea.'

'Okay.' His voice floated up to her through the louvres at the back of the house.

'Where are you?' She walked through the shadowy kitchen to the top of the back steps.

'Out back.' Andy was crouching down near the back wall of the house. 'There's room down here to store things, if you need.'

'What?' She came down a few steps and looked around, then froze. 'Hey, what are you doing?'

Andy rattled the latch. 'It's stuck.' He stooped right down to peer through a gap in the warped batten wall. 'Nope. Nothing in there. Just dirt.'

'It's just the crawlspace. Gross. Leave it.'

Andy stood up and grabbed the sliding bolt with both hands, leaning his weight against it. It popped, throwing him back onto his arse.

Marlene cackled while Andy sat there, dazed. Then he slowly got up, pale face blushing pink as he rubbed his behind, and hunkered down to get a good look inside. 'There's a wooden pallet inside here, on the ground near the door. Might be good for storage.'

'Alright, whatever. Chuck the toolkit on it and get out of there. Wait—hang on.' Marlene went back inside and grabbed the bouncer off the couch. She brought it back out and handed it to Andy. 'We won't be needing this for ages—may as well stick the baby crap down there, too.'

'There's some big pile, right up the back. Bags of dirt or something.' Andy straightened up and came over to take the bouncer, turning it upright, thoughtfully stroking his hand across the crocheted netting. 'Stinks. Shouldn't we cover this with a sheet or something? Keep it clean?'

'There's an old tarp in the bottom of the boot—chuck that over the lot of it.'

'Okay.' Andy looked up at her, the flicker of a new idea crossing his face. 'You're going to be a good mom, Marlene. You and the baby are going to be happy here.'

Marlene squinted at him, suspicious. In her world, no one hardly ever said anything nice without wanting something. But there he stood, lanky and open-faced, the afternoon sun slanting across the backyard and catching his light brown eyes so they glowed clear and gold. 'Yeah, alright. Just go get the tarp.'

She plodded back into the house, smiling, a foreign calm in her chest.

'Hey, Paulie.'

Marlene smiled at him, standing on the stoop, tall and muscled, freshly shorn so close that his scalp showed pink through ochre stubble, leaching colour into the muggy sunset air.

Marlene stepped forward and took a deep whiff, then moved aside to hold open the screen door. *Mmm.* He smelled like red licorice.

Andy, dressed in work pants and his best t-shirt, did an unconscious soft-shoe shuffle in the lounge room. Marlene squinted encouragement at him. *Just follow the plan.*

'Hi, Paulie? I'm—I'm Andy.'

'Hey, Andy. All ready for the big day, are ya?'

Andy's eyes boggled for a moment. He swallowed and mumbled, 'Sure.'

'Come through, Paulie, we're just making tea.'

'What's on the me'n'you, then?' Paulie cracked a cheesy grin and reached for Andy's hand.

Andy stared blankly for a second, then startled. 'Oh, right.' He placed his paw in Paulie's grip and sent a questioning glance to Marlene. 'Um, what was that—you and who?'

'On the *menu.*' Marlene's jersey shirt-dress had rucked up over her boobs, and she yanked it back down. 'It's a joke—me'n'you—get it?'

'Oh, yeah. Sorry. Ha.'

'So, is she any good, mate?'

Marlene ran her thoughts along the delicious double edge of Paulie's banter. Andy would never pick up on anything. Look at him, standing there blinking like he needed to sneeze, trying to tug back his hand. She sucked in a quick breath as she saw them linked together. They could have been looking in a funhouse mirror—both tall and slim, with a hint of jaffa in their skin and hair and eyes. Paulie's auburn hair was cropped short and he was more tanned, with muscles like potatoes, while Andy's lank hair and long arms hung thin and awkward as stale French fries.

An image flashed through Marlene's mind: Paulie beneath her, Andy behind her, every crevice of her filled with their twinned gristle.

'I bet she's great in the kitchen.' Paulie shot Marlene a wink. 'Noodles again, Marls?'

Was that a crack? 'Fuck off.'

'Aw, come on. What's it gonna be?'

'Ma showed me how to cook something special for tonight. You're the first person to come over for dinner in my new place.' Marlene turned away, heading into the kitchen. 'Wanna drink?'

'Yeah, ta. So, mate, for real now,' Paul asked Andy. 'What's this special dinner gonna be?'

'Noodles,' Andy deadpanned, oblivious.

Paulie wheezed a laugh through his teeth, and followed Marlene into the small kitchen. She saw him take it all in: cracked brown and mustard lino, wobbly little table fenced with odds-and-ends chairs. She liked the image she presented in that dim, grimy kitchen. She made Paulie feel superior, and that was alright with her. In fact, it was perfect. And it was temporary. He'd find out soon enough who was boss.

She bent down into the fridge, curved her spine, and looked up to lock eyes with him. Opened her lips a little wider than necessary. 'Beer?'

The tip of Paulie's tongue had poked out of his mouth, playing with the pale patch of stubble he nurtured under his bottom lip. His eyes were smoked glass.

Marlene smirked. 'Beer, then.' She grabbed a tallie and a Cruiser, clanking them on opposite sides of the narrow tabletop.

Andy quietly slipped behind them, cracking open the fridge to get a can of home-brand cola. 'What's next, Marlene?'

'You done the meat?'

'Yes.'

'Is it all brown, like Ma said?'

'Yes.'

Marlene glanced at the list of instructions pinned to the fridge door by a AmaSecure promotional magnet. 'Have you added the vegies?'

'Um, no.'

'Well, add the vegies then, brainiac.'

'These ones?' Andy picked up a frozen bag, covered in pictures of pre-cut mixed veg. 'They're frozen solid.'

'Yep. Ma said just dump 'em in, they'll melt straight away.'

Marlene raised her eyebrows to Paulie. 'He's a fucking scientist, and he can't remember three things in a row.'

'A scientist? I thought you said he worked with compu—', Paulie hesitated, the light flickering a second too late.

'A *computer* scientist! Ha, got ya, haha.' Laughter gurgled in Marlene's chest.

A few minutes later, Andy spread three bowls out next to the stovetop. 'Alright, then. Yeah, it's ready.'

Marlene jumped up and grabbed two of the bowls. 'Right— drinks, forks, here we go.' She placed a bowl at her place, and one in front of Paulie. The meat and veg was all colourful against the yellow noodles, glistening with peanut oil.

'Yum. Looks good.' Paulie smiled, first at Andy, then at Marlene.

They all took turns plopping see-through red sauce on top of their food, mixing it around with their forks. Paulie took the first mouthful, chewed a few times, then slowed, looking surprised.

Marlene watched, her face tight with worry. Would their plan work?

Andy was chewing away as Paulie started spitting out colourful little lumps into his fingers. Marlene took a quick mouthful.

Soft noodles, chewy beef strips, not bad. Sauce maybe tasted a bit weird. But it was alright so far. She took another forkful. Bit down on something rock hard and stone cold.

'Fuck!'

Andy jumped in his seat. 'What's wrong?'

'Fuck it, the vegies are still frozen. Gross!'

'Oh, I'm sorry, I'm sorry Marlene. Here,' Andy leant over to take her bowl, but she slammed her hand down on his wrist.

Paulie winced, then looked at Marlene with wide eyes. 'Don't worry about it, it's not that bad.'

She flicked him a reassuring smile, then hissed at Andy. 'This. Meal. Is. Fucked.'

'You'll start a new trend.' Paulie tried for a joke. 'Noodles with little vegie ice blocks—it's a bonus.'

'Yeah, right. We can't eat this—it's not even cooked. It'll give us food poisoning or something.'

'What about—' Andy's whole frame shuddered with a deep in-breath. 'What about if we get pizza instead, Marlene? You like pizza, right?'

Paul chinked his beer against Marlene's empty Cruiser. 'Hey, great idea!'

Andy pushed his chair back, taking the chance to move out of Marlene's reach.

'Let's get pizza.' Paulie smiled, showing those blunt fangs.

'Pizza?' Marlene swivelled her gaze from Paulie to Andy and back.

'Yeah. What do you reckon, Marlene?'

Andy pressed himself into the corner of the bench, making as small a target as possible. 'Marlene likes extra pepperoni.'

She took a slow, broken breath, her shoulders jerking as she sighed it out. 'Meatlovers.'

'Yes, yep.' Andy nodded like his life depended on it. 'Meatlovers, extra pepperoni, no capsicum. Paulie?'

'Whatever. Meatlovers is fine.'

'Sure sure, okay. I'll order, then clean this up.'

'I'm going to the loo.' Marlene pushed back her chair and left for the bathroom, refusing to look at either of them.

'Okay, great.'

When she returned, Paulie was looking in the fridge. She checked around, and heard Andy tapping away in the next room, muttering pizza toppings to himself in a weird little chant. Marlene pressed her mound up against Paulie's backside. 'More beer?'

Paulie did a slow salsa, grinding his hips back into her, then stood and turned around. His eyes were on the open doorway to the lounge room, but his hands went straight to her breasts. 'Mmm, beer's always good. On a hot night.' He dropped one hand to pull her hips against his hardening cock, and ran his tongue hungrily down her cheek, gaze still on the door.

'Pick up or delivery?' Andy's voice from the next room made them leap apart, stirring up a blast of fridge air.

She chuckled softly as Paulie dashed behind a chair to hide his crotch. 'You should go get it, Andy, after stuffing up the meal.'

'Go get it?' Andy poked his head into the kitchen. 'But I can't drive.'

'Can't drive, mate?' Paulie looked at Andy like he'd just announced he had a terminal disease.

'Course he can drive, he just doesn't have his Australian licence yet. That's how come I mostly drive his car.'

'Get it delivered.' Paulie suggested. 'Let me chip in.'

Andy Morse-coded a quick look to Marlene, then answered. 'Actually, it'd be great if we could use your card. Mine's maxxed out until pay day.'

'But we can give you the cash—it's still our shout.' Marlene slowly ran her thumb under the bra strap that had slipped down her shoulder, settling it back into place, keeping her eyes locked with Paulie's.

'Sure.' Paulie pulled his wallet out of his back pocket but stayed put behind the chair. Marlene shared a secret smile with him, then stuck out her hand for the card. He handed it over without even looking, tossing his wallet onto the table next to his phone, and reaching for his beer. Marlene passed the card to Andy.

'Here you go.' Another shared, secret smile, this time with her fiancé.

'Thanks.' Andy's head disappeared. Marlene took a seat and pointed for Paulie to do the same, then kept him occupied with inane bitching about work. She could hear Andy typing, and then she caught the quick scrape of his handheld reader skimming the card. Her shoulders crept up a notch in excitement.

They were still speculating about whether old Mr Koroma would beat Marlene out of Paulie's job when Andy came in and placed the card on the table. Paulie slipped it back into its narrow leather slot.

Marlene stood, taking Paulie by the hand. 'Let's go to the lounge so Andy can clean up in here.'

'Sure.' Paulie grabbed his beer and followed Marlene out, leaving his wallet and phone behind.

Andy flicked the wallet open. Paulie's face stared up at him, unsmiling, from a Queensland driver's licence. Andy ran his eyes over the identifying data: licence number, address, date of birth.

It was Andy's turn to smile.

Later that night, Andy lay on the couch, body long and quiet, head resting in Marlene's lap. The TV showed grizzly close-ups of a woman's body, clothes shredded and bloodied, then the scene cut to a bunch of overly manicured faces pretending to care. Free-to-air was entertainment Russian roulette, all barrels loaded.

Marlene's fingers twirled in his hair. 'So, did it all go okay?'

'Yeah, it was easy once you gave me his card. It's in the system now, ready for when he goes.'

'We did good last night. Lucky neither of us can cook for shit.'

'Yeah, lucky.'

She tapped him lightly on the forehead, her hand open and soft. 'That was a smart plan, I guess.'

'Really?'

'Pretty smart, for sure.' Marlene's eyes glittered. 'Getting cocky, aren't ya?'

The muscles around Andy's mouth quivered. 'Naw, you did most of it, Marls. That Paulie, he'd believe anything you said. You were totally in charge.'

'So much in charge that I had to basically do a strip tease in the kitchen to distract Paulie while you got his card?'

'Oh, right.' Andy flushed. 'Sorry.'

'Yeah, see? Maybe not so smart after all.' She pumped the volume on the crime show.

He slowly let out his breath. Maybe she'd let it go.

They watched the show for a while. Marlene's stomach burbled against Andy's ear, acid juices chomping through the pizza. Apparently, a human was growing in there, too; cells multiplying and dividing, like a micro-bunch of tightly packed grapes.

Andy checked the time. Eleven o'clock. Still plenty of time for KorSpace. He'd make an instant coffee with three scoops. His knees twitched, preparing to move.

'Oh, no you don't,' Marlene's hand on his brow hardened, pressed.

'I said I'd meet the posse at—'

'More computer games?' Marlene's lips slowly protruded in a thoughtful pout. 'Well, I guess you've earned some downtime. You've been working hard.'

Andy flicked his gaze back and forth from Marlene's face to the door of the study. 'Really?'

She took her hand away from his forehead, lifting it high as if granting a Presidential pardon. 'Yeah, baby. You go do what you need to do. We can have Couple-Time later.'

Andy forced a smile. Marlene's idea of Couple Time was sporadic and unpredictable. Once, she made him cross the tracks at the Rocklea shunting yards to prove he loved her. He sprained his ankle jumping down from the platform, clumsy with terror at the eight-line expanse between them, noisy and crowded with carriages in various states of coupling. Another time, she drove them to Jolly's Lookout and there above the night-black bush vista she vacuumed his whole soft penis into her mouth and pressed a bent knuckle deep into his butthole, all the while schooling his fingers in how to jitter and poke between her legs. They stayed like that for hours, it seemed, conjoined across the handbrake, Andy's eyes rolling back in his head with each new sensation until his temples ached and his cock burned.

Andy slid off the couch. 'Okay, *oll korrect*. Ha. Thanks, Marlene.' He slunk into the study and fired up his computer. Tonight's session was pivotal to his plans for his posse. He zoned out the sound of the television and sank into KorSpace, his pulse and breathing gradually settling into the same steady beat.

An hour or so later, something caught his attention, pulling him away from the concentrated effort of coordinating his posse as they installed and synched new framepacks. The television blasted ads in the next room. He leaned back in his chair, craning to check if Marlene was calling him, but the lounge room was empty.

That weird tapping sound started up again, right under his chair. He rocked his feet from ankle to toe like a paranoid airplane passenger. This house was probably filled with massive tropical termites. An image squirmed into his mind of worms with teeth eating their way up through the floorboards, through his shoes, into his flesh and bones.

A series of chat messages bleeped. lunajonny had forgotten to back up before installing the framepack—again—and was in a panic. Andy dove back into the game, funnelling expertise through his fingers into the ether, his feet writhing awkwardly on the dusty floor.

Sahil took forever to come back this time. Andy fidgeted, knitting with invisible needles, waiting. His whole system was jammed on high, strung out and jangling. It was only twelve-thirty, but he was weirdly exhausted from the effort of keeping his voice calm, his movements smooth.

Today was the day. Sahil was all over the place: distracted and clumsy, making errors through his shift all morning, logging in and out multiple times for unscheduled breaks. It was the perfect time for Andy to slip a fake account into the system.

He glanced at Sahil's coffee cup. Tiny shreds of rotting ham were barely visible, mixed in with the oily dregs from his super strong espresso. Andy took the cup to the kitchen and rinsed it out carefully, using hot water and a plastic brush dripping with detergent, then left it in the sink, filled with water and bare of prints.

Soon after Andy got back, Sahil walked slowly up the

corridor and dropped into his seat, his forehead greased with fever. 'You better drive, Andrew.'

'Okay, sure. I'll just note the change.' Andy opened up the job log, angling his body to shield the screen. He keyed in Sahil's programmer ID instead of his own, then entered his passcode and nudged Sahil. Sahil didn't even focus on the screen, just typed his passcode in, burped, and reached for his water bottle.

Andy closed the job log. 'I'm going to update the customer account data before we test the new merge, okay?'

Sahil groaned quietly. 'Sure, whatever.' He put his elbow on the desk, leaning his cheek on his fist so heavily it closed his right eye.

Andy downloaded the customer database on screen one, then opened the reporting code on screen two. He clicked the cursor onto a backdated line in screen one, then hovered it over screen two, artfully pointing his face in that direction so Sahil's bleary vision tracked the target screen.

But out of his peripheral vision, Andy checked screen one as his left hand snapped Ctrl+V and pasted the new data he'd preloaded—full name, date of birth, street address, Driver's Licence, Medicare number, account codes.

And there it was: Paul Devon, Premium Service account, buried among the pile from last month when a customer drive led to a spike in new accounts. Easy.

'Set to merge?'

'Set to merge.' Sahil mumbled.

He started the operation and watched as the report code ate into the new customer data, cross-checking before searching and confirming banking details, setting up auto-transfer permissions, disabling alerts. Information flowed across the screen like gold dust. When it was finished, Andy would have complete access to Paul Devon's identity, to do with as he pleased or required. Instead of smiling, Andy jerked his jaw back and forth a few times.

Sahil slumped, his dull eyes on screen two, ignorant of the crime being committed, in his name, right in front of his face.

·  ·  ·

In KorSpace, Chubers Bar 'n' Grill cranked out a muzak mishmash of country and cabaret. GrinreepR threaded around the hokey tables with lunajonny, waiting for word from DatPwns. A hallucinatory mix of AI avatars milled around them; chatting, smoking, fighting and dying, oblivious.

GrinreepR smashed a rack of bottles, points exploding from the shelf.

lunajonny played along, firing off a shot that nearly clipped GrinreepR.

lunajonny: haha!!

GrinreepR turned and blasted him. lunajonny stayed down for a full minute as GrinreepR bobbed over the transparent avatar, waiting. As it turned solid again, they squared off for a moment. A message blinked up onto the game screen.

DatPwns: guys I'm stuck out here

GrinreepR lowered his weapon, and lunajonny followed suit.

Andy hummed a happy tune. It was time. He tabbed out across the partition in his hard drive and fired up an old account he'd stockpiled way back when he was a newb, tooling around with version V1 of KorSpace.

A memory flickered: his skin grey as the peeling walls, a teenager at his computer in an six-by-eight trailer bedroom, axel yawing as his sister earns the rent. When it goes quiet Dale creeps out to check on her, bent like a wire on the rotting couch by the kitchenette, but Sally turns her face away. The foldout chair on the porch squeaks as their mother rises to greet the next john mounting the steps. Dale disappears back into his room, quietly latching the door.

And there it was: the lit fuse.

A hunger for the pay-off burned in adult Andy's gut. He loaded the old V1 KilKor beast into the current game, then jumped the partition again. One click to load the play-through camera that would capture every moment of the game, one more click to start recording.

GrinreepR and lunajonny charged out the saloon doors side by side. Achachak saw them coming.

DatPwns: where you been???

lunajonny raced to his side, throwing flames at Achachak's mount.

GrinreepR ran straight past them, instead throwing out a shield to protect Achachak from stray fire.

lunajonny: what the fck?!!!

Achachak aimed the red crosshairs at DatPwns' head, a sure kill.

DatPwns: shit shit shit help

lunajonny: wtf double cross? run DatPWNs
RUN!!!!

But it was too late for DatPwns. The last of his stash bled out with each pulse of the assault. His avatar hit the ground, faded, and disappeared. Achachak's stash glutted like a pig.

lunajonny turned and ran, too, heading for the safety of Chubers.

GrinreepR fired his weapon. The blast caught lunajonny mid-stride, locking him in a little-known glitch. Achachak strolled up beside GrinreepR, and slowly raised his blaster. GrinreepR turned away and left him to it. He strolled around behind Achachak's mount and stood out of harm's way.

Then, Andy tabbed through the partition and woke the beast.

The old V1 graphics seemed pot-holed against the slick version V5.3 setting, pixels blending and jerking. The KilKor shimmered into the fray, sneaking right up behind Achachak just as he finished off lunajonny. Another huge slug of kredit boosted Achachak's stash.

The leaderboard popped open, top left, a real-time report of Achachak's new Top Ten rank.

Andy glanced once then shut the leaderboard down, clearing his screen of distractions.

A crowd of curious avatars had gathered at the periphery of the battle.

> Achachak: you there GrinReepR? come get ur kred

Andy smiled to himself. Achachak really believed ten thousand units would be enough?

The KilKor stepped out from behind Achachak, and then right over the top of him so that the two images blurred into one. Achachak started spinning, slowly, while the crowd watched. Hundreds of avatars pressed in closer as Achachak spun faster and faster. The avatar quivered as it spun, pixels breaking off, bursting like fireworks. The momentum grew and grew; the crowd pressed closer and closer.

This was it. Andy's heart burned in his chest. His thumb hovered above the space bar for a second, then fell.

*Boom.*

Achachak imploded. A black hole swirled, sucking in every avatar on the scene. Hundreds of them, hurtling into the haze, starburst pixels streaking the lunain.

The leaderboard popped open again. Achachak showed up dead, his account wiped, along with hundreds of other players. And at the very top of the board, a new patch of robot vomit: fonts and spaces that made no sense, as if the current leader ran on an account the system couldn't read.

Andy didn't wait to see the board change. He flicked off record, saved the vid, and uploaded it to the play-through site on his AnOn channel, then shut everything down.

Let the world watch. Let them try to figure it out.

And all that kred was just sitting there now, safe in his old Kor account, where he could transfer it across bit by bit to GrinReepR, or whoever he chose to be next. A new account, a new name, another chance.

.  .  .

The last Sizzlers standing spawned a queue out the door and through the carpark. Marlene waited impatiently, tapping her fingernails on Da's wheelchair, her pink and gold spandex-lace dress tight as a wetsuit. Her brand-new husband stood still and quiet beside her, sweating but handsome in black drill trousers and a pink business shirt. She gave him an encouraging smile—his eyelids flicked uncertainly before giving her a small flash of teeth back.

Juny and Stevo were behind her, fielding Ma's complaints about the Registry chapel. The pair were obviously feeling some kind of survivor guilt, as they should, at having had their own fancy-pants wedding all bought and paid for.

'How about all the flowers but, hey Ma? They were so nice and didn't cost us a cent.'

'Hff. No lilies—no sons.'

'Lookin' forward to a feed, Mrs H? Can't go past good ol' Sizzlers, I reckon.' Stevo rubbed his six pack, swaying his back like a pregnant lady. 'Mmm, cheesy bread here I come.'

Ma eyed the restaurant façade dubiously, from asphalt walk to faux-wood gable emblazoned with the once-landmark red and green sign, now shabby, overpowered by the forest of fast-food banners that clustered around this hub of the six-lane Ipswich arterial. 'Why does it always look like Christmas here?'

The queue inched forward. Marlene jittered like a kid waiting for her turn on the jumpy castle. She couldn't bear another minute before her wedding feast began. Turning abruptly, she pushed the chair towards the ramp. 'I'm gonna see what's happening. Meet youse at the top.'

'Hang on, love.' Terry gripped the brake lever. 'Let me walk it.'

'You okay, Da?' Junette came forward, hooking her arm under his elbow.

'Of course I'm alright, Juny, for God's sake!' Terry snapped. 'I walked you down the aisle. After that bloody rubber-stamp ceremony, the least I can do is walk meself into Marly's wedding dinner.'

'Lunch,' supplied Andy. 'It's lunchtime.'

'You takin' the piss?'

'No, sir.'

'Come on, Andy.' Marlene beckoned. Da had been taking shots at Andy all morning. She directed her husband to Da's free arm as he teetered in front of his chair. 'Make yourself useful.'

'I can *do* it.' Terry shook like a wet dog, nearly overbalancing as he cleared himself of Junette and Andy's helping hands. With fragile dignity, he drew his lopsided spine erect and crooked his arm in Marlene's direction. 'Daughter, dear?'

'Aw Da, you're such a weirdo.' Marlene was delighted, stepping forward to take her father's elbow and parade slowly up the ramp. Juny dumped her handbag into the chair and rolled it up behind them, Stevo following. Marlene turned to check on Andy. He eyed Dionne uncertainly, then extended his pointy elbow to her. She took it without any fuss, and they brought up the rear.

Da managed to convince the young guy at the counter that he would fall down and have some kind of fit if he didn't get a table, pronto. So before she knew it, Marlene was seated next to her husband, with her family gathered around, at the table right next to the buffet.

They polished off a couple of courses, and then Da clanged his beer glass with a fork. He slid back his chair as if he was going to stand, but Ma put her fine fingers on his withered forearm and whispered something in his ear. He glanced around, and leaned heavily on the table as he pushed himself to standing, saying loudly, 'What's the world coming to, if a man can't make a bit of a fuss at his eldest daughter's wedding?'

'Marlene, my darling girl, you're a woman now and married to this young man, come along to take you away from us. Haha, no, I'm joking—come to take you into your own future, I guess. And over the years, since you were just a little baby, I've always tried to protect you and look after you as best as I could,' Terry's voice caught in his throat, and he took a sip of his beer. 'We've always tried to do the right thing by you, and you've turned out strong and determined, just like your Mother,' he rested his hand fondly on Dionne's shoulder, 'and that's the best we could've hoped for. I wish you every blessing for a long and happy life, together. So now, let's all raise our glasses and drink a toast on this special day, and wish them all the best as they start life and a family together—here's to Marlene and Andy, A.K.A Mister and Missus Walker.'

Marlene's cheeks were hot and tight with joy: everyone was looking at her like she'd won Oz Lotto. She watched proudly as they drank to her future; under the table, she shared her excitement with Andy, squeezing her nails into his thigh. After a life of mischief and misery, Marlene finally felt like a solid citizen.

Junette sculled off the last of her wine and plonked her glass loudly on the table. Marlene smiled indulgently. Any excuse to get her party on, that Juny—she'd always been that way. 'Speech!' Juny yelled. 'Come on, Andy, let's hear something from you for a change.' She broke up laughing at the look on Andy's face and waved him to his feet.

Stevo joined in. 'Come on, it's your wedding day, mate—hit me with your best shot! How's it feel?'

Andy slowly pushed back his chair and examined everyone around the table with a detached gaze. Marlene's stomach roiled in anticipation. She silently urged him on, not sure if Andy could rise to the occasion, but desperately wanting him to impress everyone with how much he loved her and how good their life would be together.

'Well now, today has been extra special, and I'm glad Marlene is having a happy day, and, well, I'm having a happy day, and you all, too.' Andy stumbled over his opening words, getting lost in among all those days and happinesses, but a gleam was forming in his eye. He opened his mouth to continue and left it flapping there for a full count of three; breath audible, cheeks flushing. 'So now, I want to say that I've got a special surprise for Marlene. She said as how she doesn't care about a honeymoon, because we need to save, but…'

Marlene glanced over at Junette, who raised her eyebrows in shared excitement, then gazed back up at Andy, rapt. He looked taller and broader to her today—more confident, somehow. Manly.

'Well, I've booked us a holiday. I got a great deal up at Cape Trib, in a safari tent place. It doesn't sound fancy, but it's comfy and real private and beautiful and, well, I hope you all think— um, I think it'll be good?' Andy looked around, seeking confirmation.

'A tent in the middle of nowhere? Bloody great honeymoon that'll be!' Marlene threw up her hands. 'Have you even *met* me?'

An awkward pause, then Juny forced out a laugh, and Stevo joined her. Marlene could feel them all waiting, worrying she was going to cause a big scene.

Instead, her face blossomed into a triumphant smile. 'Haha, only kidding youse! It sounds awesome—Cape Triv, here I come!'

'It's Cape Trib, dummy,' said Juny, laughing for real this time.

Marlene felt her cheeks flame and fell silent. She glanced at Andy, whose mouth flopped open and closed like a fish.

The air around their table stilled for a moment.

'Whatever, sis. A surprise honeymoon—how about that?' Marly gave Junette a friendly punch to the shoulder. 'See, isn't he a good one?'

'Yeah, sure is. Nice one, Andy!'

'Well done, mate,' chimed in Stevo. 'Smooth move!'

Andy sat down, clearly relieved, and Marlene enfolded him in a bear hug. 'Oh, baby, you've done really good by us.'

He patted her shoulder and gave a distant smile.

Terry kept staring at Marlene, as if he'd only just met her but liked what he saw. He waited until the fuss died down a bit. 'I reckon that's a good thing, a really good thing. I'm happy for you, the both of you.' He glanced at Andy, smiling. 'When do you go?'

'I booked it for tomorrow afternoon. Gives us time to pack and do a few chores around the house.'

Terry nodded and smiled again.

'Leaving on a jet plane,' Junette sang, tuneless and upbeat, holding out her glass to Stevo. 'More wine, please. We gotta celebrate!'

'Um, actually, I've booked us on the train…'

'How long you going for?' Even Dionne was looking cautiously pleased with the turn of events.

'Two weeks, ma'am. It's out in the forest, so we'll be out of touch.'

'Make sure you take some pictures!'

'Juny, it's their honeymoon!' Stevo feigned shock.

'Oh, gross, not those kind of pics!' Junette laughed, elbowing him in the ribs. 'Hey, we'll come around in the morning and help you pack!'

Marlene and Andy exchanged a quick glance. Marlene spoke up. 'Are you kidding? Um, thanks, but I think we'll be right.'

'Juny, you're hopeless. They just got married!'

'Oh yeah, ha! Sorry. Alright sis, we'll see you when you get back then.'

'Hold your horses, now, they're not disappearing just yet. We haven't even finished eating.' Terry broadcast a smile around the table. His face looked fuller, younger, as if years of pain had been lifted away. He got up and went around behind Marlene's chair, rested his lame arm on her shoulder and stuck out his other hand to Andy. 'Good on you, son. Welcome to the family.'

Andy blushed dark pink, clashing against the dusky rose of his shirt. 'Oh, okay then.' He stood and shook Terry's hand.

Marlene pushed out her chair and stood between them, reaching up to sling an arm around each of their necks. 'My two big strong men, hey? Come on, let's go do some damage to that dessert table.'


'Wanna watch TV?' Andy had done his research. He had the wedding night all planned out: a complex decision tree had taken root in his mind, all branches leading to one single outcome. Pills from Terry's medicine cabinet in his pocket.

Marlene's favourite pillow next to him on the couch. 'CSI is on, with that guy you like—the one you call silver fox.'

'Hmmph. But we need some special Couple Time, baby.' Marlene came close, her hand stroking his face, moving down onto his chest, popping the buttons on his shirt. 'You know how important it is, right? Especially after you've gone and made a big surprise plan for us and everything, without even telling me.'

'Yes, Marlene.'

'But don't worry, I've got a big surprise for you, too. I've come up with something super-special for tonight.'

'What's that?' Sweat prickled Andy's palms.

'You just wait.' She stroked his face one last time, ending with a light slap on his cheekbone, and disappeared into the bedroom for a few minutes. Andy checked his watch, recalculating the night's busy agenda. Depending on what Marlene had in mind, he might even be able to turn this change of plans in his favour.

When she came back, Marlene was wearing a black mesh nightdress that was cut thigh-to-titty on each side. A bright red rose was embroidered over one breast. She stood in the doorway, one hand hidden behind her back and the other stretched up to rest her elbow on the jam. She thrust one leg forward, and waggled her foot at him, sliding it side-to-side across the nylon carpet. 'You like?' She flaunted red-painted toenails.

'Yes, Marlene.' Andy knew what he had to say, even though the scene before him was celluloid-thin and translucent, his mind far removed.

She frowned at his crotch. 'I said, you *like?*'

Andy took a sharp breath and sat up. 'Yes, Marlene. You're very sexy.'

'Well, let's have some fun, then.' She slunk towards him, drawing the hidden hand out from behind her back and slowly unwrapping her fingers. In her palm lay a shiny bottle of slut-red polish, and a large set of compound-lever nail-clippers. 'You're getting real cheeky lately, aren't you? Big ideas, big man.'

The skin crawled on Andy's balls, snailing them up tight into his groin.

'Well, I like a man with a feminine side, too. You know? So, I'm gonna give you pretty nails for the holiday, just like me.' She held up the other hand, twisted her wrist and twinkling her fingers. 'You like my pretty nails, don't you?'

'Um, yes.' Andy swallowed a hard lump of tension. 'They're very pretty.'

'You like the colour, don't you, my sweet Yanky robot.'

'Oh yeah, red and super, um, super sexy.'

'You are going to get super-pretty nails, too, my husband.'

'Me?' He tucked his fingers under his knees, curling the tips protectively. 'But—do I have to? I need my fingers for—'

'Yeah, you do have to.' Her voice turned all business, rough pebbles skimming from her lips. 'It's meant to be sexy, dickhead. Here.' Marlene grabbed an empty pizza box lying on the floor, plumped down next to him on the couch and balanced the nail polish on the armrest. She slinked her fingers over the patchy velour cushioning. 'Now, lie down, baby. Lie back and relax.'

Andy lowered his butt onto the couch and rested the back of his head tentatively in Marlene's naked lap. Sweet perfume cloyed his nostrils, making it hard to get enough air. His senses swam. She put the pizza box on his torso, smoothing it flat. 'Nice and steady. Now.' She ran her fingers down his forearm and gripped his right hand, lifting and laying it on top of the box, patting it into place. 'Let's start with the pinky.'

At the first snip, Andy flinched.

'Stay still, baby, or this will Take. For. Ever.'

He braved a glance down at the procedure. A gibbous moon of newborn pink exposed the quick of his little finger. She worked efficiently across both his hands, then reached for the red polish.

Andy tried to keep his voice calm. 'Marlene, how about I get you a drink first?'

III.

The gunmetal snake coiled in its throne. It had taken to lying in wait, here in this yellow woven basket suspended above the dirt, ready to strike at any movement below.

There were two shapes down here this night, two companions, instead of just the one thick, crawling sausage of stink the snake had grown accustomed to. Two shapes, but only one moving—awkward, slow, thumping and scraping, clumsy in the dead of night.

Terry groaned as he lowered himself down on to the worn cotton sheets next to Dionne.

'Big day, today.'

'A big day, yeah.' Terry scratched his fingers through his beard. He felt better tonight, somehow. Stronger than he'd felt in many years. He let out a loud, rough sigh. 'But a good day, eh love?'

'You in pain? You need something extra tonight? I can get them for you.'

'Nah, nah, I'm alright.' He lay back on the pillow, turning to rest his good arm on his wife's slender hip. 'You alright?'

'Of course, I'm alright.'

He stroked Dionne's silken skin, his heart swelling with

peace and love and pride and something he couldn't name. The
he felt a movement between his legs, a quickening.

Lust.

For the first time in decades, Terry's arteries firmed with the
vital rush of desire. Of longing. Of life.

Dionne's age-smudged eyes shone with joy. As one, they
reached for each other, moving softly out of the past to hold
each other close in shared surprise, and gentle hope.


'It's too hot for the garden, son.' The old guy next door would
lean over the broken-down wire fence.

'We're going away for a while—better do it now, or it'll never
get done.'

'You and the missus taking a holiday, huh?'

'Yeah, heading up north.'

'Well, that manure's been sitting there ever since I gave it to
old Sam, before you even moved in. Good to see it put to good
use.'

Andy would stab the point of the shovel into the woven
plastic bag and brown stink would burst free, cascading onto the
dead grass. 'Yep. I'll do the whole place, and then just wait for
rain.'

The neighbour would raise his long, stubbled chin and
examine the skyline, looking for all the world like a weathervane
mounted on a barn. Straight up the sky would be hard and blue,
but over the mountains black clouds would boil in a distant,
purple sky. 'You won't have to wait long, I reckon.'

'Better get stuck in then.'

Andy would work through the afternoon, racing the clock.
He'd be exhausted from the long preparations the night before.
As usual, Marlene would prove a handful. His packed bags
would stand by the door, ready to grab and go.

The house would be eerily silent. Just like he liked it.

Job done, he would shower off the muck, run clippers
through his hair, check the mirror.

Nod to himself. *Hey there, Paulie.*

Then he would pull on his black runners and conduct one last walk-through of every room. Nothing of his left, and nothing out of place.

Under his feet, a new mound of dirt would decorate the crawlspace. He pictured it, nestled beneath the faded yellow bassinette, hidden by the tarp. He thought he might go and check it, one last time. Maybe put an open bag of manure under there, in case all the stuff on the garden didn't throw neighbours off the scent.

Night would fall, deep and swift.

Paulie would check his watch. No time. He could trust himself to have done a good job down there; he would have made sure everything was in order. He would step out onto the porch and lock the door, just as the bus rounded the corner. A dozen quick strides and he would be at the stop, hand out in a confident hail, hydraulic brakes yelping like a struck dog as the bus pulled over. He would nod to the driver.

'Airport link, thanks mate.' His new Aussie accent would be spot on.

The driver would nod without even looking at him, leaving Paulie to take a seat near the rear door, his mind as focussed as if he had a keyboard in his hand.

*Oll korrect, all clear, okay to proceed.*

As the bus took off, the clouds above them would burst, thunder rumbling and rain sheeting down, heavy as sin. But the brand-new Paulie would ride the bus with scrubbed hands and a light heart, oblivious to everything but the bright promise of this, his next chance.


Eyes crusted shut. Throat full of mudcrab claws. Fingers welded into hooks.

A shaken breath rattles cracked ribs.

Alive.

The flesh of her hands knotted and ripped to shreds, Marlene stretches out a toe. Encounters cloudy softness under a layer of grit. And then, a waxen slab.

She forces her hands into motion, lifts them to her bruised lips. Spits. Rubs stiff knuckles across her eyelashes, loosens the glue, and forces her eyelids apart. It is dark here, but not too dark. Grey shapes in sepia tones, jumbled as nightmares.

Rust. Sodden pools of rust, caked with grey-brown dust.

Spattered.

Andy.

The wax lump, long and thin beside her in bed, as he was meant to be for the rest of her life. As he had been, for the balance of his.

She flinches at a flash of memory from last night. Drugged, suffocated, but not yet bound. Strong enough. She had been strong enough. She pulled him into pieces with her bare hands. She gouged and fought and so did he. But as she held him down in a final moment of choice, a change came over him. For the first time since she'd met him, Andy got talkative. Yelling at first, then pleading, then explaining. Every detail painted with clarity. His mother. His sister.

His real name.

She shuts her eyes, then rubs them opens. It wasn't lying dead beside her, proof of her decision made. Not her Andy, with his neck awry, snapped out of alignment with his weak spine. She stares at him, fighting the undertow of unconsciousness. Loses the fight, submerging through layers of adrenalin and opioids. Layers of memory.

Her father.

A shadow with a blade.

Open flesh gushing red waterfalls.

A gunshot.

Fury brings her back to consciousness; a fierce, focussing rage.

Her parents have protected her, all this time. Ma, with her earnest face full of lies. Da, shouldering in silence the burden of his broken will. They have loved her, maybe even loved her best, all along.

They will protect her again, there is no doubt.

And Andy had made such beautiful plans: detailed and

thorough as ever. Plans that would work just as well for Marlene.

The stolen identities: he is no one. How can someone who is no one ever be missed? Marlene groans herself upright, reaching for his leg. Gives a firm yank, testing its mass. The corpse shifts easily. A lightweight.

The money. She eyes his backpack, tucked neatly next to the bedroom door, ready for his departure. His laptop will be in there, for sure, packed full of information. Her husband taught her well enough how he ran his scams—he needed her to lure in the next mark. And what he hadn't shared, she had spied from her observation posts under the house. She is sure she'll be able to track down at least some of the stash.

And then, the compost. Brilliant. Yes, her husband, whoever he had been, had planned things well.

But it is Marlene who survives.

She flexes the chunky muscles across her shoulders, along her arms. Bends her thick legs and slides off the bed into a squat. Her new belly pooching, she slowly pushes to standing. The pain forces open her mouth, but she does not make a sound. Everything about her body is now within her control. Her mind too, turns and catches the light at her bidding. She is connected up inside in a way that no one will ever tear apart again.

She throws the crumpled doona on the floor, anchors herself against the end of the bed, and grips her husband's ankle. Her would-be widower hits the floor with a muffled thump, obscure even in death.

Marlene drags the load towards the back door: her final visit to the crawlspace she knows so well.

# ACKNOWLEDGMENTS

Thanks to all the people who helped this story come in to being, including Kim Wilkins, Peter M Ball, Joon-Yee Kwok, Rebekah Turner, Emily Craven, Kate Eltham, and Lois Spangler—all awesomeness is theirs, all errors mine.

And to my family: Luke, Declan, and Griffin—thank you for all your love and support.

*To the lion-hearted third-culture kids from my boarding school days; and,
to Phil, who died a hero.*

# ABOUT THE AUTHOR

Meg Vann writes twisted mysteries to thrill readers seeking to make sense of the world's injustices. Meg is also a respected industry leader and cultural producer who works across writing, editing, publishing, bookselling, and festivals. She lives in a ramshackle Queenslander  with her loving partner, delightful sons, and devilish rescue chihuahua.

facebook.com/megvannwriter
instagram.com/lilac_lioness

THANK YOU FOR BUYING THIS
BRAIN JAR PRESS CHAPBOOK

To receive special offers, bonus content, and info on
new releases and other great reads,
visit us online at www.BrainJarPress.com

www.ingramcontent.com/pod-product-compliance
Lightning Source LLC
Chambersburg PA
CBHW030843200726
48285CB00007B/2534